Elizabeth Blackwell

Girl Doctor

Illustrated by Robert Doremus

Elizabeth Blackwell

Girl Doctor

by Joanne Landers Henry

ALADDIN PAPERBACKS

First Aladdin Paperbacks edition 1996
Copyright © 1961 by the Bobbs-Merrill Company, Inc.

ALADDIN PAPERBACKS
An imprint of Simon & Schuster Children's Publishing Division
1230 Avenue of the Americas, New York, NY 10020

Designed by Antler & Baldwin, Inc.
Manufactured in the United States of America

18 20 19

Library of Congress Cataloging-in-Publication Data
Henry, Joanne Landers.
Elizabeth Blackwell, girl doctor / by Joanne Landers Henry. — 1st Aladdin
Paperbacks ed.
p. cm.
Originally published in 1961 under the title: Elizabeth Blackwell, girl doctor.
Summary: The life of the first woman doctor in the United States, who
worked in England and America to open the field of medicine to women.
1. Blackwell, Elizabeth, 1821–1910—Juvenile literature.
2. Women physicians—United States—Biography—Juvenile literature.
3. Women physicians—England—Biography—Juvenile literature.
[1. Blackwell, Elizabeth, 1821–1910. 2. Physicians. 3. Women—Biography.]
I. Title.   R154.B623H46   1996
610'.92—dc20   [B] 95-33496 CIP AC
ISBN-13: 978-0-689-80627-8 (Aladdin pbk.)
ISBN-10: 0-689-80627-2 (Aladdin pbk.)
0311 OFF

To my parents

Illustrations

Numerous smaller illustrations

Contents

Elizabeth Blackwell

Girl Doctor

The Strawberry Man

SEVEN-YEAR-OLD Elizabeth dried her hands and carefully folded her hand towel. She hung it beside the tin washbasin which stood beneath the playroom's broad bay window.

She looked at the other towels hanging alongside hers. "One, two, three," she counted, "and mine makes four. One each for Anna, Marian, Samuel, and me. When the little ones—Henry, Emily, and baby Howard—are old enough to leave the nursery, there will be seven!"

Mother had to spend much of her time in the nursery with the younger children. The playroom was for the older children. Here they did

11

their lessons, and here they romped and played together when the weather was bad.

Elizabeth, who was fondly called "Bessie," was glad there were so many children in the family. There was always someone to play with, and there were always exciting things to do.

With a thrill, Bessie thought of what this morning promised. "Today I'm going to the marketplace. And Mother said I could buy some strawberries for us to have at teatime!"

Of course Bessie knew she could not go alone to the market place. Miss Major, the young governess or teacher, and Bessie's older sisters, Anna and Marian, were going, too.

Mother had given Bessie the copper coins to pay for the berries. She had wrapped the coins tightly in a handkerchief, then pinned the handkerchief securely at Bessie's waist.

Bessie felt the coins in the handkerchief. Then she stood on her tiptoes. Through the open bay window she looked down into the courtyard one story below. She leaned far over the washbasin. There were the graceful purple lilacs and white jessamine her mother had planted.

"How lovely England is in June!" thought Bessie. She took a deep breath of the early morning air. It smelled sweet and fresh. It was not yet clouded with dust from the great city's busy streets and many factories.

At the far end of the walled courtyard stood her father's sugar refinery. Father, she knew, was one of Bristol's richest merchants. Their house was one of the finest in the city, but people looked up to Father for another reason.

Mother said Father was a reformer. He believed in equality for everyone—rich men, poor men, black or white.

"Even children have their rights!" Father would thunder. "Girls should have the same education as boys."

13

"Samuel's ideas are too advanced for 1828," Bessie heard her Aunt Bar say one day. "Whoever heard of boys and girls going to school together? And studying the same subjects, too! No good will come of it, mark my words."

Bessie was puzzled by what her aunt said. She liked having Miss Major as their teacher, and it was fun to go to school in the playroom at home.

Other children, she knew, went away to boarding school. But Father said that in these schools the girls were not given the same subjects as the boys. He felt that his children would be better off at home with a tutor to teach them.

Suddenly the quiet of the playroom was broken. "Please hurry, Bessie," lively twelve-year-old Anna called. She was the oldest of the Blackwell girls. Miss Major said Anna was a very good student, though a little headstrong.

"Yes, do hurry!" echoed Marian, as she followed Anna into the room. Marian was the dreamer, Aunt Bar said. She claimed that that was what made Marian's head ache so often. Father laughed when he heard this.

"We must get to the marketplace near Bristol Bridge as soon as we can," Anna said urgently. "If we are late, all the berries will be sold."

Bessie nodded. But first she had to finish buttoning her dress. She fingered the row of tiny buttons under her chin.

"I'm hurrying," she put in, working to get the buttons fastened. Her small fingers moved quickly. At last all the buttons were done.

Anna's and Marian's bonnets were neatly tied under their chins. Their stiff white pantalets showed a few inches below their skirts.

Smoothing her skirts, Anna turned toward the door. "We'll wait for you downstairs, Bessie," she called over her shoulder impatiently.

"As soon as I put my bonnet on I'll come," Bessie replied somewhat stubbornly. She was eager to see the bustling marketplace. But she was de-termined to dress herself, even if her sisters did have to wait.

Rapidly she pulled her bonnet on over her straight flaxen-colored hair. As she was about to tie the ribbons, Miss Major came in.

With a smile she bent down to Bessie. "Here, let me tie your bonnet for you, Bessie," she of-fered. "Bows are so difficult!"

"No, thank you, Miss Major," Bessie answered firmly but politely.

Miss Major shook her head and laughed. "Though you are tiny, you are most independent! I should remember that you always want to do everything for yourself."

Bessie smiled at Miss Major's gentle teasing, but she didn't stop working. After several tries, she got the bow tied to her satisfaction. "Now I'm ready, Miss Major!" she announced, her blue-gray eyes sparkling.

She and Miss Major joined Anna and Marian downstairs. Soon the large gabled Blackwell house was out of view.

Bessie was thrilled with the new sights on this morning's walk. Usually the girls took their daily walks in the afternoon and along quieter streets.

Happily she skipped ahead of her two older sisters. The puffed sleeves of her light summer dress bobbed as she went along. Her tiny slippers, tied with crisscross ribbons, tapped lightly on the walk.

The sun was shining brightly now, but an earlier shower had left muddy pools in the narrow, winding streets. Carts and wagons rumbled by as the girls approached the river that linked Bristol with the sea.

"Are we near the market place by Bristol Bridge, Miss Major?" Bessie asked eagerly.

"We haven't far to go," Miss Major answered. "Do be careful of the traffic now!" she warned.

17

As they rounded a corner and turned onto a still more crowded street, a great black carriage drawn by two lively horses thundered past.

"Look out!" Anna cried. But the warning came too late. *Splash!* The hem of Bessie's dress was covered with mud.

"Oh, dear!" Marian cried. "What will Aunt Bar say, Bessie?" She looked at Bessie's spattered dress and mud-spotted shoes.

The four Blackwell aunts lived with them. Aunt Bar helped Mother with the children. She taught them their manners and scolded them when they misbehaved. When they did something wrong, she wrote it down in her little black book. She said the Black Book would help to remind the children of their bad deeds and teach them to behave better in the future.

Bessie loved Aunt Bar, but sometimes felt that she was awfully strict. "Maybe," Bessie said hopefully, "she won't put me down in the Black Book this time. It—it was just an accident." With a worried frown, she looked up into Miss Major's kind face.

Miss Major smiled. "I expect Aunt Bar will understand, my dear."

"Yet," Bessie added thoughtfully to herself, "sometimes it seems that I just can't help getting into trouble."

Bessie soon forgot her accident. There were

too many new things to see and too many questions to ask Miss Major for Bessie to think about her muddy clothes.

Just ahead of them now Bessie could see housewives and maids arguing with the farm women over the price of butter and eggs. She noticed that almost all the country people were women. "Why?" she asked Miss Major.

"Most of the farmers stay at home on the farm and do the chores," Miss Major explained. "So the women—wives and daughters—bring the food to market to sell."

Bessie stopped by the first countrywoman she came to. The woman sat on a low stool by a large basket. Eagerly Bessie looked into the basket. There were nice white eggs and some delicious-looking creamy butter, but no berries.

"Don't you have any strawberries to sell?" Bessie asked, disappointed.

"Ay, no, young miss!" the woman answered.

"I had only a few baskets of berries, and I sold them early this morning."

Quickly Bessie went on to the next country-woman, and the next. Each one wagged her head "No" in answer to the question.

Now straight ahead of Bessie was Bristol Bridge. Nearby was the place where the farmers brought their cattle to sell. Fascinated, she stopped to watch and listen. In white smocks, the drovers, or cattle dealers, made their cries heard above the street noises and the cattle.

Marian was not so bold as Bessie. She stayed close to Miss Major's side. Anna tried to keep up with Bessie, though she sometimes found this a difficult task. Bessie hurried tirelessly from one spot to the next.

At last Bessie suggested, "Let's cross the street. Maybe I can find some berries over there." She tried to sound hopeful, but she was beginning to feel discouraged. Perhaps because of her

21

they had been too late in getting to the market-place after all. "Oh," she said to herself, "I just can't disappoint Mother."

Marian and Anna wanted to give up the search, but Miss Major was willing to go on a bit farther.

Bessie acted quickly. She looked both ways before she crossed the street. When she saw the way was clear, she plunged on eagerly. Miss Major, Anna, and Marian followed her.

Nimbly she wormed her way through the crowds. But she had no better luck here than she had had on the other side of the street.

"Oh, dear!" Bessie thought. "I suppose I should give up, but I want to keep trying."

Once again she looked around to see if her sisters and Miss Major were nearby. She could see that they were not far behind. She hurried on to the next countrywoman. This one was young and gave Bessie a big smile.

"Would you like some nice fresh eggs, Miss?" she asked.

"No, thank you," Bessie replied, "but I must get some strawberries. Do you know where I could buy some?"

"Well, there was an old man here. His basket was not far from mine." The young country-woman hesitated a moment. Then she said, "I'm nearly certain he had some berries to sell."

Bessie's eyes sparkled at the good news.

"But he drove off in his cart a few minutes ago," the young woman added. She turned from Bessie and looked down the busy street. "There he goes now." She pointed toward the bridge.

Eagerly Bessie tried to pick the old man out. There! She could just see him as he drove toward the bridge. Several times she nearly lost sight of him in the crowd. What could she do?

Bessie decided quickly. If she was to have the berries, she must stop the old man.

23

Without waiting for her sisters or Miss Major, she dashed off. She ran as hard as she could.

She was so determined to catch the old man that she didn't feel the ribbons on her bonnet work loose. Suddenly the bow came untied and the bonnet flew off behind her. Bessie didn't notice. She could see the old man very clearly now. She had almost caught up with him.

"Please stop, please stop, Strawberry Man!" she cried as loudly as she could.

The old man turned and saw the little girl racing after him. He tugged on his donkey's reins, and the cart came to a stop.

"What can I do for you, young lady?" he said kindly when Bessie reached him.

"Oh, I'm so glad I reached you in time!" she managed to say at last. "I want some strawberries—for my mother."

The old man reached around and took a small basket of berries from the cart. He handed them

to Bessie. "What a lucky thing I had this one basket left!" he said with a chuckle.

Despite her mud-covered dress and shoes and the lost bonnet—which she had just discovered missing—Bessie was happy. She had managed to find some berries for her mother.

She unpinned the handkerchief from her waist and gave the farmer the coins. Then she thanked him and skipped off merrily toward the cattle market. She could see her two sisters, followed by Miss Major, hurrying to meet her.

"I have them—I have them!" Bessie called excitedly, as they drew near one another. She held the basket of berries high for them to see.

Anna and Marian hid their faces in their hands when they met Bessie. Their shoulders were shaking with laughter.

"You are a sight, Bessie!" Marian said.

"Indeed you are!" Anna added. "But at least we'll have berries to eat today."

When Miss Major joined them, she had Bessie's lost bonnet in her hand. She scolded Bessie for behaving in such an unladylike manner. But her tone softened and she smiled when she saw how happy Bessie was.

"Your dress and shoes are a bit muddier than they were before. You even have a few specks of mud on your face. But I'm sure we'll be able to brush the worst of it off when it dries. I'll see to the bonnet myself."

"Thank you, Miss Major," Bessie said gratefully. "From now on I'll try to remember that I'm a lady."

"You must promise me not to be so reckless in the future," Miss Major went on.

Bessie smiled at the governess. "I promise," she vowed.

Doctor Bessie

"OH, I DO wish I had this hem finished!" Bessie thought to herself. She frowned as she looked at the linen napkin. Slowly, carefully, she took a stitch—then another, and another.

"If I could finish before Anna or Marian, I could be the one to help Mother in the nursery. But I just *can't* sew any faster!"

Bessie sat on a cushioned stool close by Aunt Mary's knees. She glanced up at Aunt Mary, who was darning Samuel's socks. It made her feel good to be near her aunt. She was round and jolly, and her eyes always twinkled.

A summer rain beat hard against the windowpanes, but the little back parlor seemed cheerful and light to Bessie.

It was a few days after her visit to the market. In the morning she and her brother and sisters had done their lessons. Miss Major taught them reading, writing, arithmetic, geography, and French. Now Aunt Mary was helping the girls with their sewing.

Suddenly Bessie's thoughts were interrupted by a giggle from Anna. "Do look, Marian, at how slow Bessie is!" Anna held up the dainty apron she had been working on. "I'll be done long before you are, Bessie," she teased.

Marian grinned. "Bessie can run much faster than she can sew. But I'm afraid you'll beat me, too. I can't seem to keep up with you."

"That's because you spend so much time looking out the window, Marian," Anna laughed.

"I'm not just looking," Marian added. "I'm making up poems—in my head."

"Now, girls," Aunt Mary pretended to scold. Then she turned to Bessie. "Let me see how you're doing, dear," she added warmly.

Bessie handed her napkin to Aunt Mary. Thoughtfully Aunt Mary looked it over. Then she smiled and nodded her head. "Yes, all the stitches are exactly the same length, and they are neat and even—just as they should be."

Bessie felt encouraged by Aunt Mary's words. "But, Aunt Mary, why can't I sew as fast as Anna or Marian?" she asked.

Aunt Mary chuckled. "You are such a serious little girl!"

"Maybe I try too hard. Maybe that's why I'm so slow," Bessie said as if to herself. "But Father says I should always do my very best."

Aunt Mary chuckled again as she gave Bessie a loving pat on the head. "You're much like your father. Why, someday you might even be as well known in Bristol as he!"

"Oh, Aunt Mary, you're the biggest tease of all!" Bessie cried with a laugh.

Then the girls went back to their sewing. Anna stitched rapidly. She didn't stop to talk or to look around. From time to time, though, Marian would pause to look out the window. The rain still beat hard against the panes.

Bessie, like Anna, did not stop. Even so, she saw that she was going to be much longer in finishing her work than her sisters.

She thought longingly of the good times she had in the nursery. It was such fun to help with the babies. Today, however, she was sure to miss this treat.

Suddenly Anna cried, "My apron is done! May I go now, Aunt Mary?"

Bessie bit her lip to keep from showing the disappointment she felt. "Anna has worked hard and fast," Bessie thought. "She has earned the right to go to the nursery today."

"Yes, you may go, Anna," said Aunt Mary, "but do be careful of the stairs. They were freshly polished this morning." Without looking in Anna's direction, Aunt Mary continued to sew.

Anna didn't wait to hear Aunt Mary's last words. She rushed from the parlor and through the hall to the stairway.

Suddenly from the stairs came a frightened cry. Then *thump, thump, thump!*

"Mercy!" Aunt Mary cried in alarm.

Bessie quickly realized what had happened. Anna had fallen on the stairs. She didn't hesitate. She jumped up from her stool and ran straight to the stairway. Close on her heels came Aunt Mary and Marian.

Bessie was the first to reach Anna. She lay, moaning, at the bottom of the stairs.

"Mercy!" Aunt Mary cried again. "Poor girl!" She wrung her hands nervously.

Marian rushed forward and stooped down beside Anna. "Oh, poor Anna!" she wailed. She stroked Anna's hair and tried to comfort her.

Bessie wasted no time on sympathy. She knelt beside her sister. "Where are you hurt, Anna?" she asked in a kind but firm tone.

"O-o-oh, my ankle!" Anna moaned. Tears came to her eyes as she looked up into Bessie's calm face.

Gently Bessie ran her fingers over Anna's injured ankle. "Maybe the bone is not broken,"

she said to herself. "Perhaps it's just sprained."
Bessie recalled the time Samuel broke his leg.
It had looked much worse than Anna's ankle.

"Oh, what shall we do?" asked Marian.

"Go fetch Aunt Bar. Hurry now," Aunt Mary
said. "Dear me!" She bent down to put her
arms around Anna's shoulders. "I warned you
of the stairs, dear Anna."

"I—I know," Anna managed to say, though
tears still came to her eyes. "I'm sorry, Aunt
Mary. I—I guess I didn't pay attention. I was
in too great a rush."

Soon Aunt Bar hustled in, followed closely
by Marian.

"Now, let me see what's wrong," Aunt Bar
said, a worried frown on her face.

"It's her ankle, Aunt Bar," Bessie offered.

Aunt Bar carefully examined Anna's ankle.
Once the young girl winced when Aunt Bar
squeezed a little too hard.

Bessie watched with great interest. "Is it broken, Aunt Bar?" she asked.

Aunt Bar shook her head. "No, but the way Marian carried on, I thought surely Anna had broken her head! It's good that you keep your wits about you, Bessie."

"I'm sorry, Aunt Bar," Marian apologized. "I—I was so startled and frightened that I couldn't think straight."

Aunt Bar turned to Aunt Mary. "We should get Anna upstairs to her bed. The sprain is bad, and she must not walk on the ankle."

Bessie looked at Aunt Bar admiringly. Everyone turned to her whenever someone was sick or injured in the family. She always seemed to know just what to do.

Slowly and carefully Aunt Bar and Aunt Mary helped Anna to stand on one leg. Anna put one arm around Aunt Bar and the other around Aunt Mary. They put their arms around Anna's waist.

Step by step they eased her up the stairs. Bessie and Marian followed. When they came to the top of the stairs, Bessie darted on ahead of them.

"I'll fix the pillows on Anna's bed," she called back over her shoulder.

Bessie, Anna, and Marian shared one bedroom. Quickly Bessie pulled the pillows from her bed and from Marian's bed. She carried them to Anna's. There she carefully arranged them at the top.

"Now," she said, giving them a final pat. "With three pillows, Anna can rest easily."

When Aunt Mary saw how neatly Bessie had fixed the pillows, she said, "Very good, Bessie. That will do nicely."

Soon Anna was comfortably propped up in bed. But Bessie noticed that Anna's ankle was swelling fast. She wondered what Aunt Bar would do for the swelling.

"Now," Aunt Bar announced, "Anna must rest. Aunt Mary, would you please finish going over the luncheon plans with Margaret, the cook?"

After Aunt Mary had left, Aunt Bar turned to Marian. "Your mother should be told about Anna's ankle. But do tell her not to worry."

"Yes, Aunt Bar," Marian replied. Then she hurried off to do as she was told.

"Could I help you, please, Aunt Bar?" Bessie asked eagerly.

"Wouldn't you rather help your mother and Marian in the nursery, now that Anna cannot?" Aunt Bar asked, surprised.

Bessie hesitated. It was such fun to care for the babies!—No, she had made up her mind. "I think I could be more useful here," she answered seriously.

"Well—I could use help. Both of your other aunts—Lucy and Ann—are gone today."

"Do let me stay, Aunt Bar," Bessie pleaded.

Aunt Bar smiled. "Very well." Then she turned to Anna and took another look at the swollen ankle. "Now, Anna, I'm going to fix this ankle up as good as new."

"What—what are you going to do, Aunt Bar?" Anna asked fearfully. "Will it hurt?"

"No, not a bit," Aunt Bar reassured her. "Bessie, you run down to the kitchen. Ask Margaret to give you some vinegar and a lot of paper. Ask her to put the vinegar in a large bowl."

Bessie was puzzled. What would Aunt Bar do with vinegar and paper? But she didn't stop to ask questions. She must do quickly what Aunt Bar had asked.

Soon she returned to the bedroom. She carried a large white porcelain bowl partly filled with vinegar. She gave it to Aunt Bar, who set it on a stool beside Anna's bed.

"I couldn't carry both the vinegar bowl and the paper," Bessie explained to Aunt Bar. "I was afraid I would spill the vinegar. I'll go get the paper right away."

Again she hurried from the room and down to the kitchen. She returned a few minutes later with four large pieces of heavy brown paper. She put them beside the bowl of vinegar.

"What are you going to do now, Aunt Bar?" Bessie asked.

"I'm going to make a vinegar compress—a pad soaked in vinegar," Aunt Bar answered briskly. "We'll put it on Anna's ankle, and in a few days the swelling will be all gone."

Aunt Bar worked rapidly as Bessie watched. She took a piece of paper and folded it several times. When she finished, she had a strip about five inches wide and fifteen inches long. She placed the folded paper in the bowl of vinegar.

"There!" she said. "When the paper is well soaked with vinegar, we'll wrap it tightly around the ankle," she explained to Bessie.

"I see!" Bessie cried excitedly. "We'll *press* it on—*compress!*"

Anna giggled. "Oh, Bessie, you have an answer for everything!"

"Laughter is good medicine," Aunt Bar said, with a smile. "But a vinegar compress helps, too. It's an old remedy—one I learned years ago. I'd nearly forgotten about it until today."

Bessie watched closely now as Aunt Bar took the dripping pad from the bowl and wrung out some of the vinegar. The paper pad was as limp as a rag.

With strong fingers, Aunt Bar wound the paper tightly around Anna's ankle. "Does that feel all right, Anna?" she asked. "The paper will hold tight until it dries. Then it must be moistened again."

"It feels nice and cool, Aunt Bar."

"You must stay very quiet," Aunt Bar warned, "until the swelling goes down."

While Aunt Bar was talking, Bessie was thinking. Perhaps her aunt would let her stay with Anna. She could change the compresses. She could be Anna's doctor!

"Dear me!" Aunt Bar sighed. "There's so much work to be done around the house. Yet the compresses should be changed often."

Bessie saw her chance. Quickly she offered, "I'll stay with Anna, Aunt Bar. I'm sure I could make a new compress, or pad, when it's needed. And I could keep the compresses moist."

Aunt Bar eyed Bessie thoughtfully. "It's a big job for such a little girl."

"Please let me try, Aunt Bar," Bessie pleaded.

"It would be such fun if Bessie could stay and keep me company," Anna added. She looked at Bessie. "I'm—I'm sorry I teased you about your sewing, Bessie. I'd like to have you here."

Bessie flashed a smile at Anna, then looked hopefully at Aunt Bar.

"Very well," Aunt Bar agreed. "Marian can help your mother, though she's not very handy with the babies. If you stay with Anna, I can finish the work around the house."

"Oh, thank you!" Bessie cried, her eyes shining. She felt proud of her job. It made her feel very grown up.

Patiently, hour after hour, Bessie changed the compresses, just as she had seen Aunt Bar do. Sometimes she read to Anna.

Bessie liked to read, and she enjoyed reading aloud. Anna helped her with words she didn't know and words she couldn't pronounce.

The next morning Anna's ankle looked much less swollen. Mother and Father came to see her as often as they could, and Aunt Bar took charge when Bessie had to go to her lessons or to meals. By late afternoon the swelling was almost gone.

Mother praised Bessie for helping Aunt Bar.

And Father said Bessie had given her patient good care. "We'll have to call you Doctor Bessie from now on!" he said with a laugh.

"Bessie did as well as I could have done," Aunt Bar added. "She has a talent for taking care of sick people."

Bessie blushed at so much praise. She was glad she had helped to make Anna feel better. "Maybe," she said to Father, "I'll be a doctor when I grow up."

"Why, Bessie," he said, smiling down at her, "I was joking about your becoming a doctor. There aren't any women doctors—not in England or anywhere! There never have been."

"Why?" Bessie asked puzzled.

"Only boys—young men—are allowed to go to medical school," Father explained. "A woman can't become a doctor. No school would let a woman study medicine."

"But that isn't fair!" Bessie said hotly.

44

"No, perhaps it isn't," Father agreed, putting his arm around Bessie's shoulders. "But if you want something badly enough, Bessie, and if you work very hard, you can get it. You have to make your own opportunities." He smiled. "Now remember this whenever you feel discouraged."

Bessie smiled back at her father. "I'll remember," she said earnestly.

A Green
Umbrella

BESSIE, Anna, Marian, and Sam crowded into the
open carriage with Mother and Father. They
waved good-by to their aunts, Miss Major, and
the younger children. It was a warm, sunny afternoon in May of the next year.

"What a beautiful day for a drive!" Mother
said, as she settled back in her seat. "Perhaps
it won't shower today after all."

With a flick of the reins, Father urged the team
of horses forward. The carriage clattered out of
the Blackwell drive and over the cobblestone
streets of Bristol.

"This has been such an exciting week!" eight-year-old Bessie thought. "And now today we're going to hear the missionary from Ireland!"

On Sunday she and her brother and sisters had gone with Mother and Father to chapel to hear the famous Scottish evangelist, Henry Craik, speak. Yesterday afternoon they had taken a drive to hear the much respected clergyman, Dr. Thomas Chalmers.

It was what Father called "Missionary Week" in England. During this week the missionaries who had come to England to visit gave talks. These missionaries belonged to Father's church. How Bessie loved to hear their romantic stories of faraway places!

"Will we be there soon, Father?" asked Bessie.

"We haven't far to go," Father answered over his shoulder. "The chapel we are going to today is just on the outskirts of Bristol."

"When do we eat?" Sam, who was near Bessie's age, wanted to know. He looked longingly at the two large picnic baskets Mother had filled with good foods.

Mother smiled. "We will hear the Reverend Mr. Brian, the Irish missionary, speak. Then we will have our picnic on the church green."

"May we go exploring first, Mother, before we go inside the church?" Bessie asked as the carriage bounced along. "I want to see everything," she added excitedly.

"If there's time, you may take a little walk," Mother answered.

Just then Father turned into a narrow lane. Behind them the lane ran downhill toward the heart of the city. But ahead of them, rising in the distance, Bessie could see a few gently rolling hills and open countryside.

Suddenly the carriage stopped. To their right was a low stone wall. Within the wall and set well back from the lane was a small stone church. Ivy climbed over the old gray stones.

A few people were walking along the lane toward the chapel. Others stood in the church-yard, talking.

Father helped Mother down from the carriage. It was not yet time for Mr. Brian to speak, so Mother gave Bessie and Sam permission to take a short walk.

"Come on, Bessie!" cried Sam eagerly. He raced off toward the rear of the chapel.

They found that the low stone wall circled all the way around the church. Beyond the wall, at the rear of the church, was a small graveyard.

Bessie and Sam were just about ready to return to their parents when they came upon an open gateway in the wall.

"Look, Sam!" Bessie pointed toward the gateway. There, leaning against the stones, was a green umbrella.

"Someone must have forgotten it," Sam said, surprised. "I don't see anyone back here but us."

Bessie looked around. Sam was right. The yard at the rear of the church was deserted except for them.

"I think we should take it to Father," she said. "Then he can find out who owns it."

"That sounds like a good idea, Bessie," Sam agreed.

"Let's hurry. We mustn't be late for the sermon." Quickly Bessie ran to the gateway and picked up the umbrella.

Together Bessie and Sam raced off toward the front of the church. As they rounded the corner of the building, they saw their family. Just then Bessie heard a shout behind them.

"Hi, there! You, stop!"

Startled, Bessie and Sam stopped running. They turned to see who had called. A short little man with a bright red beard ran toward them. His long black coat flapped as he ran. He waved his arms wildly as he called to them.

50

"Oh, dear!" Bessie said, alarmed. "What could be wrong?" She had forgotten all about the green umbrella, which she clutched tightly in her hands.

"You wanted us, sir?" Sam asked, frightened, as the man reached them.

The red-bearded man was out of breath from running so hard. His eyes flashed as he stared hard at the two children.

"You have snatched my umbrella," he said, jabbing his finger in Bessie's direction.

Shyly Bessie looked up at the stranger. Now that she took a closer look at him, she saw that he was not nearly so frightening as he had seemed at first. Why, he was almost smiling!

By now, Father, followed by Mother and the girls, had joined Bessie and Sam.

"Are these fast-acting youngsters yours, Mr. Blackwell?" the stranger asked. Then he threw back his head and laughed.

With a smile, Father shook hands. "Yes, Mr. Brian, they are. I hope they haven't been into any mischief."

Embarrassed, Bessie blushed. Sam dug his toe into the ground and hung his head. "So this is the famous Irish missionary!" Bessie thought.

The Reverend Mr. Brian bowed to Mother and the girls. "No, it was just a misunderstanding," he said kindly.

He explained to Father that he had been resting against the stone wall behind the church. He had propped his umbrella in the gateway, so that he wouldn't forget it.

"The children didn't know I was there, of course. I was on the opposite side of the wall from them."

Though Bessie felt very shy, she knew she should apologize to Mr. Brian. "I—I'm sorry, sir. I didn't mean to keep your umbrella. It—it looked lost, and I was bringing it to Father."

"You did the right thing," Mr. Brian encouraged her. "But you certainly led me a merry chase." Then he threw back his head and laughed hard again.

The grownups chatted together for a few minutes. Then Mother asked, "Could you join us for dinner tomorrow night, Mr. Brian?"

Bessie, Anna, Marian, and Sam looked eagerly at the missionary.

"What fun it would be to have him visit our house!" Bessie thought. She had heard Father say that Mr. Brian told very funny stories. He did seem very gay.

"I'd be delighted," Mr. Brian said enthusiastically. "Now it's time for my talk to begin. I will look forward to tomorrow." He bowed low to Mother and shook hands with Father. Then he hurried into the church ahead of them.

"Oh, dear!" Bessie cried, as Mr. Brian disappeared inside. "I still have the green umbrella!"

Together everyone burst into laughter.

"I'm sure the missionary won't forget his meeting with you, Bessie," Father said with a smile. "It will make another funny story for him to tell when he leaves us. Now we must remember to return the umbrella after the service."

The following afternoon, Bessie, Sam, Anna, and Marian were in their playroom. The younger children were taking their afternoon naps in the nursery.

"But why can't we have dinner tonight with the grownups and Mr. Brian?" Sam was asking. He gave his ball a kick and sent it, bouncing, into a corner.

"Because," Anna answered firmly, "you *know* we never eat dinner with the grownups. It—it's just not done in England."

"We always have an early dinner—up here in the playroom," Marian put in. She rested her chin in her hands and gazed dreamily out the window. "But what fun it would be to eat with the grownups just once."

Bessie ran after the ball and tossed it back to Sam. Suddenly she had an idea. "Why don't we ask Mother and Father if we might come to dinner, too?" Bessie recalled what Father had told her a long time ago. "You have to make your own opportunities," he had said.

"That's a wonderful idea, Bessie!" cried Sam.

"Oh, how exciting!" Marian said as she bounced up and down.

"It would be fun," Anna agreed.

"You ask Mother and Father for us, Bessie," suggested Sam. Anna and Marian added their approval.

Bessie thought hard. The dinner was a special occasion, she reasoned. So she would plan to make her request to Mother and Father in a special way. She would write them a note!

Quickly Bessie set to work. She found a piece

of paper and pen and ink. She sat down at the large low table in the playroom. Then she started to write. Carefully she formed each letter, working slowly so as not to blot the ink. At last she was finished.

Critically she eyed her work. She wanted to be sure she had done her very best.

"What did you write, Bessie?" asked Sam. He and Anna and Marian crowded close to read over Bessie's shoulder.

Bessie read the note aloud. " 'Dear Mother and Father: We would like to have dinner with you and Mr. Brian. We promise to sit quietly and behave well. May we come? Respectfully, Anna, Marian, Sam, and Bessie.' "

"Oh!" Marian cried, clapping her hands. "I hope your plan works, Bessie."

Anna smiled. "Your note sounds very grown-up, Bessie. I'm sure that Mother and Father will be impressed with it."

"Hurrah for Bessie!" shouted Sam.

Bessie blushed. She hadn't expected so much praise from her brother and sisters. "I—I'm not sure my plan will work, but I've tried my best."

At teatime, late that afternoon, Bessie delivered the note to Mother and Father. She was delighted when they told her that the children had permission to come to the dinner.

Perhaps, Mother suggested, if they behaved well tonight they could join the grownups at dinner more often.

That night a special table was set for the four children in the dining room. It was close to the big table. From where she sat, Bessie could see and hear everything. How exciting it was!

At first Mr. Brian and Father talked mostly about politics. Though Bessie didn't understand everything they said, she listened to every word.

"Times in England are growing worse," Father said with a worried look on his face. "The poor workers here in Bristol scarcely have enough money to buy bread."

Mr. Brian shook his head.

"To make matters worse," Father went on, "the government will not change its old ways. It will still permit only a few men to vote."

"It's certainly different in America," Mr. Brian said. "There every man can vote."

"Yes," Father agreed. "In America there seems to be equal opportunity for all—rich or poor."

"I've heard rumors in Bristol," Mr. Brian said. "Some say that if conditions don't improve, there will be violence—rioting."

"I sincerely hope not," Father said, shaking his head. Then he smiled. "But we should talk of happier things. Please tell us some of your funny stories, Mr. Brian."

Soon the serious subjects were forgotten. Mr. Brian told one funny story after another. The children laughed till tears ran down their cheeks. Even the servants couldn't help laughing at the funny little missionary.

It was a wonderful evening, Bessie decided as she crawled into bed that night. And what a wonderful place America seemed to be! Tomorrow she would ask Miss Major if they might learn more about America in their school studies.

The Stowaway

TEN-YEAR-OLD Bessie held tightly to Emily's hand. Emily, who was five, was her youngest sister. Bessie had promised Mother that she would watch her little sister closely. Now the two of them hurried after Father, as he led the way along Bristol's busy waterfront.

Several large sailing ships were anchored at the wharf. Father explained that these ships carried passengers and cargo to far-off countries. There were smaller boats, too. Many of these, he said, were fishing vessels. Some were tied close to the large ships. Others were anchored in the Avon River, which led toward the sea.

Bessie liked to close her eyes and pretend she could see the short way down the Avon to the mouth of the Severn River. This wide body of water, she knew, emptied into the still wider Bristol Channel. The Bristol Channel, then, spread out into the Atlantic Ocean. And way across the Atlantic was America!

Bessie had read about America in her schoolbooks. So when Father said he was going down to the waterfront on business, she begged to go along. She hoped to see one of the ships that sailed to America.

Emily tugged on Bessie's hand. "May we go to see that boat?" she asked, pointing down the wharf to a large ship.

Bessie looked down into Emily's broad face. Her reddish hair curled out from under the edges of her bonnet. Bessie smiled. "Perhaps—later on. But we must hurry now. We don't want to make Father late."

Bessie stayed close behind Father. "How easy it would be to get lost down here!" she said to herself, as she took a firmer hold on Emily's hand.

Soon Father turned off onto a narrow street not far from the wharf. When he came to a large red-brick building, he stopped.

"My business is at this warehouse," he told Bessie. "I'll not be long, so you may wait out here. Remember, though, stay close by so that I can find you easily."

"Yes, Father," answered Bessie.

As he turned to go inside, Emily caught hold of his coattails.

"What do you want, little one?" Father asked.

Emily pointed to a ship anchored at the wharf. "Is that boat going to America?" she asked.

"Yes, Emily, it is," Father answered with a smile. "In fact, it is going to leave today. Perhaps it will leave while we are down here. But no more questions for now. I must hurry."

"Oh, how exciting it would be to see the ship sail for America!" Bessie thought to herself.

After Father left, Emily begged Bessie to walk down the lane. She wanted to get a better view of the big sailing ship. Bessie, too, was eager to get a closer look. What fun it would be to go on board! Bessie knew, of course, that this wouldn't be allowed. Only passengers and members of the crew could board so close to sailing time.

Emily skipped gaily ahead of Bessie as they walked back toward the corner of the lane. Bessie glanced over her shoulder, in the direction of the warehouse. If she and Emily did not go beyond the corner, they would be well within sight of the warehouse doorway. At the corner they would be able to see the water front.

Suddenly Bessie realized Emily was too far ahead of her. Now Emily had gone a bit beyond the corner. She was going onto the wharf!

"Emily—Emily, wait!" Bessie shouted.

But Emily didn't hear Bessie's call.

"What if I lose her!" Bessie thought fearfully. She started to run. She must catch Emily before she got lost in the bustling waterfront crowd.

"Emily!" called Bessie again, as she reached the corner of the lane.

Just then a large wagon, loaded high with bales, rumbled by in front of her. For a few minutes her view was completely blocked. She lost sight of Emily. The rattle of the iron-rimmed wagon wheels on the paving stones drowned her calls to Emily.

Quickly Bessie darted around behind the wagon. But when she reached the other side, there was no sign of her little sister.

Hastily Bessie looked in all directions. Emily had disappeared!

"Oh, dear!" Bessie cried. "What shall I do?" Her heart pounded with fright.

"I must act quickly before Emily wanders too

far off," Bessie thought to herself. "If I go back to call Father, I'll lose time."

Bessie studied the wharf. Nearby were two large stacks of baled goods. Here and there were large barrels piled high on one another. Wagons drawn by horses were being loaded and unloaded. Sailors worked to get the cargo on the big ship for America.

"Maybe someone saw her," Bessie thought to herself. "Perhaps one of the sailors saw which way she went."

She swallowed hard. If only she had the courage to ask one of the men about Emily! "I must ask—for Emily's sake," she told herself.

There was a sailor near by. He was rolling a heavy barrel toward the ship.

Bessie hurried to him. "Did you see a little girl in a green dress go by?" She looked up into the man's weather-beaten face.

He gave her a quick, broad grin. "No, lassie,

I didn't." The sailor spoke with a strong Scottish accent. "Now what would a wee little girl be doing down here? And all by herself?" He leaned against the barrel and smiled down at Bessie.

"She's my sister Emily, and I'm afraid she's lost," Bessie answered in a worried tone.

The sailor raised his eyebrows. "Ay, that's too bad! Maybe the mate, that officer over there, saw her." He pointed to a man standing near the ship's gangplank. The gangplank was like a little bridge that ran from the wharf to the ship.

"Your sister could be almost anywhere down here on the waterfront." The sailor shook his head. Then, sounding more cheerful, he said, "Maybe she's just playing a game and hiding from you."

"Oh, I hadn't thought of that! But I must hurry and find her." Then suddenly Bessie had a frightening thought. What if Emily was on board the

68

ship to America? And what if she didn't find her in time—before it sailed?

With a quick "Thank you," Bessie left the sailor and ran to the mate.

The mate was shouting orders to the sailors who were loading the ship.

When Bessie spoke to him, he looked down at her through heavy black eyelashes. "What can I do for you, Miss?" His tone was gruff yet kindly.

"I'm looking for my little sister who's lost." Bessie described Emily to the mate. "Have you seen her?" she asked hopefully.

The mate rubbed his chin and looked thoughtful. Then he grinned. "Yes, I think I have." Then he slapped his knee and laughed.

"Come with me, young lady," he said. Without explaining, he took Bessie's hand and led her up the gangplank.

Suddenly Bessie found herself on the deck of

the big sailing ship. She felt the deck rock gently under her feet as the ship lay at anchor.

"Oh, dear!" Bessie thought to herself. "Is Emily really on board the ship after all?"

The mate led the way toward the rear of the ship. "This is called the stern," he explained to her. "The passengers' cabins are below deck."

Just then they rounded a large pile of rope. There, looking very much at home, was Emily in the arms of an officer.

With a happy cry, Bessie rushed toward them. "Emily!" she called.

Emily gave Bessie a big smile. "You may put me down now, Captain," she said politely.

"Very well, my little stowaway!" He laughed as she slid from his arms and ran to meet Bessie.

"I'm sorry, Captain Manning," the mate said. "She followed two of the passengers on board. I thought she was their little girl."

"I understand, Mr. Jenkins." The captain

nodded. "No harm done. We met shortly after she came on board." His eyes twinkled as he listened to Bessie's story of how Emily got lost.

When Bessie finished, he said, "I was just about to take your little sister ashore. But I would have had a hard time finding your father. The waterfront is a very busy place!"

"I came to ask the captain if he would give us a ride to America," Emily put in.

"But Emily!" said Bessie, "America is a long, long way off."

"Yes, indeed!" The captain smiled. "It takes about six weeks to sail from Bristol to New York City."

"Now you must promise never to run away and get lost again, Emily," Bessie scolded. "Mother and Father would be very anxious."

"But I wasn't *lost*," Emily said with a pout. "*I* knew where I was. And I wasn't going to leave without telling you. You know I wouldn't leave

71

without you. I asked the captain if he would take you, too."

Bessie laughed. "Oh, Emily, I just can't be angry with you! Now we must hurry back to meet Father. He will be terribly worried if he can't find us."

Bessie thanked Mr. Jenkins for his help. Then she thanked Captain Manning for his kindness.

At the gangplank, Emily turned and waved good-by to the captain. "Someday maybe I will sail to America with you!" she called.

As Bessie and Emily reached the warehouse, Father came out the door. "My business took longer than I thought it would," he said. "I hope you aren't tired by your long wait."

"Oh, we had fun!" Emily interrupted. "We had an adventure!"

Bessie hoped Father would not be angry when she told him what had happened. Quickly she explained the mishap.

At first Father frowned. But when Bessie told him that she had acted as fast as she could to find Emily, he smiled and nodded.

"You used your head, Bessie, and did what you thought best," Father said. "I can't be angry with you for that. But this little girl," he went on, turning to Emily, "must learn to think before she acts."

"I—I guess I didn't think that I was really running away from Bessie," Emily said, ashamed. "I supposed that she knew where I was. I'm sorry, Father. I'm sorry, Bessie," she added.

Bessie smiled and took Emily's hand as they turned and started for home.

"From now on, Bessie," Emily said after a while, "I'm never going to run away. I'm going to be your shadow!"

A Glow
In The Sky

"Is IT SAFE to take the girls into Bristol, dear?"
Mother asked Father. "Anna and Marian could
miss one drawing lesson."

The family was gathered round the breakfast
table. The deep-set windows of the old farmhouse were opened wide. The fresh, sunny Octo-
ber air made Bessie eager to be outside.

She loved the old thatch-roofed farmhouse at
Olveston. The family had spent the summer
here, away from the heat of Bristol. Several
times each week Father went into the city.

Since Olveston was only nine miles from Bristol, Anna and Marian went in once a week with

Father to take drawing lessons. Bessie preferred to spend every minute she could in the country.

"We've heard rumors of trouble among the workingmen before and nothing came of them," Father answered. "I'm sure Bristol will be as safe today as it has been these past months."

"What's dangerous about Bristol?" asked nine-year-old Samuel.

"Well, son, the rumors are that the laborers, the workingmen, will cause trouble," Father said. "Many factory owners do not treat them fairly. The men must work long hours for very little pay. They do have reason to be angry."

"May I go with you today, Father?" Sam asked, his eyes bright with excitement. "Then if there is any trouble, I can help protect Anna and Marian. May I, Father?"

"Me, too!" six-year-old Henry put in.

"Oh, Henry!" Marian giggled. "You're a dear, but much too little to help."

"Now that's enough." Father laughed. "I'm certain that there's very little real danger. I haven't heard a word of complaint from any of my men at the sugar refinery."

"Of course not, dear," Mother said. "You treat your men well and pay them a fair wage. But you must remember that you are the only factory owner in Bristol who does!"

"Now don't worry, Mother," Father said gently. "We will be all right. We should be leaving soon, however, or the girls will be late."

Bessie hoped that Father was right—that there was no real danger in Bristol. She couldn't help wondering, though, if her sisters and Father were wise to make the trip today.

After Father, Anna, and Marian left for the city, Bessie decided to walk through the woods and down to the brook.

Emily asked if she could go. "I want to study nature, too," she said in a serious tone.

"Aw, you don't even know what 'nature study' means, Emily!" teased Henry.

"I do, too!" Emily cried, stamping her foot. "When I study nature with Bessie, we learn all about the trees and flowers and insects and birds and everything outside. So there!"

"Now, children," Mother scolded. "You must not quarrel."

Then Bessie invited Henry to come along. He said importantly that he had other things to do.

Bessie smiled. "All right. Let's go, Emily. It's a wonderful day, and I'm sure we'll see a lot of beautiful trees in the woods. The fall colors are lovely."

Happily Emily joined Bessie. But as they set out, Bessie wondered again about Father, Anna, and Marian. Perhaps they should have stayed home. Maybe the city wasn't safe after all.

Late that afternoon the children, Mother, and Aunt Bar gathered for tea.

"Isn't Father home yet?" Sam asked, as he joined the family.

"No, he isn't," Mother answered in a very unnatural tone.

"I'm sure there's nothing to worry about," Aunt Bar said firmly. She turned to Sam. "More than likely, your father has been delayed by some business at his sugar refinery."

"Or maybe there was a fight in Bristol today!" cried Henry, his eyes shining with excitement.

"Mercy!" cried Aunt Bar. "What an awful thing to imagine, Henry."

"What if Henry's right?" cried Emily.

"Humph!" Aunt Bar frowned. "The trouble with this family is that it has too much imagination." She shook her finger at Henry. "Anna spends perfectly good time writing stories, and Marian writes poems by the hour. Now you've started to make things up just to frighten us all."

Henry's face turned red. "I—I didn't mean to

frighten anyone. But Miss Major says it's good to use your imagination."

Mother smiled at Henry. "Miss Major wants you to use your imagination in the right way. Use it to see something good or to make something worthwhile," she told him gently.

Yet, despite Aunt Bar's firm tone and Mother's smile, Bessie was still frightened. It wasn't like Father to be late. He was always on time.

Another hour passed, but still there was no sign of Father's return. Bessie saw the worried look on Mother's face. As it drew near dinnertime, even Aunt Bar began to look worried.

Mother tried to sound cheerful at the dinner table. Bessie knew Mother would not want the younger children to worry about Father and the girls. She did her best to keep the conversation light and gay.

"Perhaps Father has business in town tomorrow and has decided to spend the night there,"

Mother said. "If so, I'm sure he'll send a messenger to us yet this evening."

Shortly after dinner, Mother sent everyone off to bed. She said she would stay up for a few hours—just in case a message should come from Father.

Upstairs Bessie undressed by the light of a single candle. The small room under the low sloping roof seemed very empty and lonely without Anna and Marian.

Suddenly the quiet was interrupted by a faint tapping at her door. Then the door creaked open and Emily, barefoot and in her nightgown, came in slowly.

"Could I sleep with you tonight, Bessie?" she asked. Large tears came to her eyes. "I'm lonesome without Father and Anna and Marian."

"Of course you may, Emily." Bessie knew just how Emily felt. "Climb into bed."

Emily quickly did as she was told.

Bessie blew out the candle. Then she turned toward the window. "I'll look down the road once more," she thought to herself, "to see if a messenger or Father is coming."

It was a clear though dark night out. The moon had not yet risen. Hopefully Bessie looked down the narrow dirt road. The farmhouse was on the edge of the tiny village. In some of the cottage windows Bessie could see glimmering lights. Others were dark.

Bessie looked beyond the village. All was black and quiet. There was no sign of a rider or of her father's carriage.

She raised her head and looked at the horizon, off in the direction of Bristol. She was surprised and puzzled by what she saw, for there in the sky was a mysterious reddish glow.

"What could that be?" she asked herself. She had never seen anything like it before. Suddenly she realized it must be coming from the city,

or very near it. Since she didn't know what it was, she was frightened. Perhaps something terrible was happening in Bristol.

Should she run and ask Mother what the strange red glow was? She glanced over at Emily, who was huddled beneath the covers in the big bed. She knew if she showed her fright, Emily would only become more upset.

What should she do? What would Father want her to do?

Then she knew what Father would tell her. He would say that she must have faith and courage. As she said her prayers, she thought of Father, Anna, and Marian. Now she wasn't afraid any more. Comforted, she climbed into bed and in a short time was sound asleep.

Early the next morning she raced downstairs. Perhaps Mother had news of Father and her sisters. When she asked, however, Mother sadly shook her head.

Then Bessie told Mother of the mysterious red glow she saw in the sky last night. "What was it, Mother?" she wanted to know.

Mother looked puzzled. "I can only think of a fire. But surely we wouldn't see a *single* fire in Bristol way out here!"

"Fire?" Bessie echoed, alarmed. "Oh, Mother, what if there was trouble in Bristol yesterday? What if there were a lot of fires? We would see a glow then, wouldn't we?"

"Now, Bessie, we must try to be calm. I don't want to alarm the other children and your aunts. I'm sure—no matter what happened—that your father and the girls are all right. We must say nothing, until we know what actually happened."

"Yes, Mother," Bessie replied. Then she had a thought. "Maybe I could learn some news down in the village. Please, Mother may I go?"

Mother looked thoughtful. "Yes, Bessie. It would be good to have some news. I know Father would have sent us a message if it had been possible to do so."

Without another word, Bessie quickly hurried from the house and down to the village. It was only a short way to the inn. Perhaps the innkeeper, Mr. Johns, would know if there was any news from Bristol.

She rounded a corner and turned into a narrow street—the main one of the village. Overhead the gables of the close-set houses almost met. A small wooden sign swung over a doorway marked "The Inn."

Mr. Johns stood by the door talking to two travelers. The travelers turned and went inside the inn as Bessie drew near.

"Good morning, Bessie!" called Mr. Johns. He tipped his hat to her and smiled. "You're out and about bright and early today."

"Yes, Mr. Johns," Bessie replied. She told him that her father and two sisters had gone into Bristol yesterday, but had not yet returned. Then she told him about the mysterious red glow.

"Has anything bad happened in Bristol?" she asked, giving the man an anxious look.

Mr. Johns shook his head sadly. "I fear there has been trouble. Those men I was talking with left the city last night. They say there were riots. The troublemakers started a good many fires. The good citizens of Bristol have been fighting the fires all night."

Bessie suddenly felt very frightened again. Then she remembered that she must have faith and courage. She threw back her shoulders and hastily thanked Mr. Johns. Then she rushed from the inn.

As she hurried home, she thought about the news she must give her mother. But she was determined to help by being as brave as she could.

Silently, hopefully, she and the family waited all day for news from Father. None came. The following day the worry lines around Mother's eyes seemed deeper to Bessie.

Again Mother tried to keep the family's spirits up. Bessie, too, did her best to encourage her sisters and brothers.

Then, without warning, late that afternoon the front door burst open. Amid shouts of joy, Father, Anna, and Marian rushed in to greet the delighted family.

Mother hugged Father. Bessie, Emily, Sam, and Henry all tried to hug Anna and Marian at the same time. Bessie felt as if she had a hundred questions to ask. But she was so happy to see Father and her sisters that she couldn't seem to do anything but smile.

At last order was restored, and with a weary sigh Father sank into the nearest chair.

"I was terribly afraid some harm had come to you and the girls, dear," Mother said. "Now we can be thankful you are home safe. Bessie's courage set a good example for the other children. She was a great help to all of us here."

Father smiled and put his arm around his daughter. "Good girl, Bessie!" he said.

"Was there a fight, Father?" Sam interrupted excitedly.

"Mr. Johns said there was rioting," Bessie put in. "Is it true?" She couldn't hold her curiosity any longer.

"Children!" Mother scolded. "Father's very tired. You mustn't bother him with questions right now."

"I'm not tired," Anna offered, her eyes shining. "I can tell the story. May I, Father?"

He laughed. "Yes, Anna. You and Marian tell the story. Your mother and aunts must be as eager to hear it as the children."

Everyone listened as Anna told them what happened in the city. At first the rioters marched through the streets, making a lot of noise.

"Yes," Marian interrupted. "They shouted their complaints and shook their fists."

Soon a large mob gathered. They grew angrier and angrier. Then the mob went to the city hall, and there they set fire to the great building. From the city hall they went to other important city buildings. They set fire to these buildings, too. All of Bristol seemed to be aflame.

The citizens who wanted to protect their property were powerless against the shouting, angry mob. No one could stop them.

Finally the mob decided to destroy the beautiful old churches of the city. One of these churches was the lovely St. Redcliffe.

"But there the rioters were stopped by a single man!" Marian cried. "And who do you suppose that man was?"

"It was Father!" Anna took up the story again. "He was not afraid of the mob."

The listeners gasped at the danger.

Anna told how Father spread his arms across the church's doors. He barred the rioters' way. Then he spoke to them and persuaded them to stop their needless destruction. Now, to all Bristol, Father was a hero!

Sam's eyes grew big. "Did you see all this happen, Anna?" he asked.

"No, of course not, silly," Anna said. "Father told us where he had been. Marian and I were safely locked in at home. But I can see exactly how it happened—in my imagination."

"Everything Anna says is true," Marian put in stoutly. "All Bristol is talking of Father's bravery. The church he risked his life for wasn't even the kind of church we belong to. But most important of all—the anger of the rioters lessened after Father stopped them from burning the church. Soon the mobs broke up, and the men returned to their homes."

Father smiled. "I'm flattered that my family thinks I'm a hero. I'm thankful that I was able to help stop the riots. I felt it was my duty to save the church.

"I'm lucky the mob spared my life—and my sugar refinery," Father went on. "But there is so much trouble in England now, I sometimes think it would be wise if we moved to America. It's a promising land—a new country with many freedoms we do not have."

Bessie had heard Father talk of moving to America before, but never so seriously. He seemed very discouraged by the Bristol riots. Perhaps now the family would go to America.

For the next few days Mother and Father spent long hours talking about America. It would be hard, Bessie knew, to leave their family and friends behind. But how thrilling it would be to live in a new land—"a land of opportunities," Father called it.

Then one day Father was given the bad news that his sugar refinery had burned to the ground. His business had been wiped out. It would take a great deal of money for him to rebuild.

"This," he said, "has helped me make a very difficult decision. Instead of rebuilding here, we will move to America. There I'll start up my business anew. And I'll try out some new ideas."

Mother had tears in her eyes, but she smiled through them as Father told the children of his decision to move. His announcement brought some tears as well as shouts of joy.

Bessie's eyes sparkled as she thought of the days ahead. How exciting it would be to board a great sailing ship and set out for a new country! What, she wondered, would America look like? What would their life there be like?

A New Land

Bessie was just barely tall enough to see over the railing of the ship.

Mother stayed below deck with the babies, Howard and Sarah Ellen. But Father and the other children had come up to catch their first glimpse of America—New York City.

Seven-year-old Henry climbed up into the ropes that ran from the railing high into the main mast of the ship. He held onto a rope with one hand and leaned far out.

"Henry!" called Father. "Get back. We don't want to lose you in the harbor."

"I can see fine from up here," Henry cried excitedly. He obeyed his father, however, and found a safer spot on deck.

Father held Emily high so she could see, too.

It was a gray September day. The air was heavy and damp, and a haze hung close to the horizon. Even so, Bessie could make out land in the distance. To the right, said Father, was a large island. To the left was the shoreline of the State of New Jersey. Straight ahead but not yet in sight was New York City.

Father explained that the Hudson River ran along the west side of the city. "That is the river to our left." He went on, pointing, "The river to our right is called the East River."

As they drew closer, Bessie saw two barges in the East River. The barges were flat-bottom boats that carried freight. Now they could see the lower shoreline of the city. At the wharfs, several other sailing ships were docked. Behind them were the many buildings of the city.

Bessie felt like some of the pioneers Miss Major had told them about. Eagerly she stared over the ship's railing. Ahead lay a new land—and adventure!

Suddenly the deck of the ship was filled with activity. The first mate shouted orders to the sailors. Some climbed quickly up the rigging and took down the great sails. Others stood by with heavy ropes to make the ship fast to the wharf. Two of the strongest sailors prepared to let out the heavy anchor.

Father put Emily down. "We will go below now, children. I must see that everything is packed. And we don't want to get in the sailors' way when they are so busy."

Reluctantly Bessie turned and followed Father and the children below deck.

Within the hour the family found themselves standing on the wharf. Their luggage was piled high around them.

Miss Major held tightly to Emily's and Henry's hands, while Aunt Bar carried Howard. Mother held Sarah Ellen in her arms. Aunt Mary, Aunt Lucy, and Aunt Ann tried to keep their eyes on Bessie, Sam, Anna, and Marian. The children were busy darting this way and that, exploring their new surroundings.

"I'll find a carriage to take us to our hotel," Father said. He looked around. "It's odd that there aren't several carriages close by. Usually cabs meet incoming ships."

Bessie, too, was puzzled. She had expected to find a busy waterfront—one certainly busier and more crowded than Bristol's. Yet there seemed to be only a few men working. The two city streets she could see leading away from the wharf were empty.

The harbor end of the wharf was blocked from view. Bessie and Sam asked Father if they could walk out to the end of the wharf. They wanted to see more of the harbor. Father said they could go, then he set off in search of a carriage.

Sam darted on ahead of Bessie. He had almost reached the end of the wharf when he gave a shout. "I say, Bessie—I've found a treasure!"

Eagerly she ran to where Sam was standing. He was near the edge of the wharf. There, behind one of the posts, was an old ball.

Bessie laughed. "It's not a very new treasure, Sam," she joked.

Sam laughed, too. He picked the ball up and tossed it high in the air, then caught it. "Even so, I can keep it. There's no one out here, so the ball must not belong to anyone."

Suddenly there came a shout from shore. Then there was the sound of someone running. Bessie and Sam turned to see who had called.

A boy, about Sam's age, ran past the luggage and packing cases and out to where Sam and Bessie were standing.

"That's my ball!" he shouted angrily.

Sam glared back at the strange boy. He was poorly dressed. His clothes were torn and dirty, and his cap was pulled down over one eye.

"Give it here!" The boy tried to grab it from Sam's hands. "I saw you from on shore—you took my ball."

Sam jerked away. In a flash the two boys were locked together in a fierce struggle. Sam broke free, but the boy came at him again. He tackled Sam around the waist, and with a thud the two boys fell to the ground, rolling over and over.

Sam let loose of the ball. It rolled away, toward Bessie. Quickly she stooped and picked it up, to keep it from rolling off the wharf and into the water.

The boys were a tangle of arms and legs. Bessie tried to think of a way to stop them. Silently, anxiously, she watched the fight.

Suddenly Sam broke free again and leaped

to his feet. The other boy followed. Fists clenched, he struck out at Sam. A blow landed squarely on Sam's left eye.

Stunned, Sam fell back, but he recovered quickly. He took a big swing with his right arm and caught the other boy off guard. His punch landed solidly on the boy's nose.

"That's enough!" Bessie cried. She was determined to stop the fight right now.

Startled, the two boys dropped their hands to their sides and stared at her.

"I have the ball," Bessie went on firmly, "and I'm going to keep it, unless you stop fighting."

The stranger stared at Sam. His eye looked red and puffy. Sam stared at the stranger. There was a trickle of blood coming from his nose.

Abruptly both boys burst into laughter.

"You Americans are good fighters," Sam said to the other boy. He held out his hand and grinned broadly.

The boy grinned back. "And you're a good sport. My name is Ted—Ted Sparks."

"And mine's Sam Blackwell. This is my sister Bessie."

"I think this is your ball." Bessie smiled and handed the ball to Ted.

Ted's face turned red. He grinned sheepishly and stared down at his feet. "I guess I shouldn't have been so quick to pick a fight."

With a look of concern, Bessie gave him her handkerchief. "Maybe this will help to stop your nose from bleeding."

Bessie turned to Sam. Gently she touched his reddened eye. "Your eye will be black tomorrow, I'm afraid. But when we get to the hotel, we can put a cold compress on it. That should help."

"Yes, Doctor Bessie," Sam joked.

Then the three of them laughed. As they started back to join the other Blackwells, Sam told Ted that they had just come from England.

Ted shook his head. "You've come at a bad time." But before he could tell them why, they reached the rest of the family.

Father had just returned. Sam's bad eye and the new boy went unnoticed. Everyone was busy listening to Father.

"There are no carriages," Father was saying. "New York is very nearly deserted."

"Deserted!" cried Mother.

"There's been a cholera epidemic," Father explained. "Many people are sick, and many have died from it. It's worse than any we've seen in Bristol. Those who could left the city to avoid the sickness."

Bessie felt uneasy, but she tried not to show it. She knew all about cholera. First came a raging fever, then sickness. Too often, there was little hope of recovery.

"Well," grumbled Aunt Bar, "we'll just have to make the best of it."

Father smiled. "You're right, Aunt Bar, and we will make the best of it. I know that the City Hotel isn't far from here. After all these weeks on the sea, a walk on land will be good for us."

"What about our luggage, dear?" Mother asked in a worried tone.

"Maybe I could help," Ted offered.

The strange voice surprised Father. He turned and saw Ted for the first time.

Sam introduced Ted to his Mother and Father, then to the other Blackwells.

"Sam and I met Ted—out on the end of the wharf," Bessie put in.

"I see," said Father, looking at Sam's red eye.

Quickly Bessie and Sam explained what had happened. Both Sam and Ted said they were sorry about the fight.

Father laughed. "Well, it's good to make friends in a new country, Sam. But perhaps after this you can find a better way! Now, how can

103

you help us, young man?" Father asked, turning to Ted.

"I know where I can borrow a handcart, sir," Ted said. "We could load your luggage on it, then Sam and I could push it."

"Great!" Sam cried.

Father thought Ted's idea was a good one. With a smile, Ted raced off to get the cart. In a very short time he came back, pushing the empty cart ahead of him.

Soon Father and the boys had the cart loaded. Aunt Mary took the baby from Mother's arms. The Blackwells fell in behind Father as he led them from the wharf.

Anna and Marian giggled. "Oh, isn't this exciting!" Marian cried.

"What an adventure!" cried Sam. As they passed along the dark, narrow streets of the strange city, he looked around. Most of the shops were closed and heavy blinds were drawn behind the windows. Except for an occasional house, shutters were tightly shut. This made the streets seem even more lifeless.

"I think it's spooky," Henry said with a shiver.

Soon they reached the city's Hall of Records. There the Blackwells saw people gathered in small groups.

"Look!" Sam stopped the handcart. He pointed to the building's entrance.

The Blackwells halted. Two men carried a stretcher toward the building. On the stretcher was a young girl about Bessie's age. The stretcher-bearers had handkerchiefs tied over the lower part of their faces.

Bessie could hear a woman crying. The people in the small groups talked in hushed tones.

"This hall has been turned into a hospital," Ted explained.

A well-dressed man passed by. He was hurrying toward the temporary hospital.

"Why can't doctors cure cholera?" Bessie cried hotly. The cry escaped her—she hadn't meant to speak out loud. But the sight of suffering and the unhappiness that came with it upset her. "It's not right!" she thought to herself.

Suddenly the man stopped and looked at Bessie. There were dark circles of weariness under his eyes. He looked pale and very tired.

"We doctors do all we can," he said.

Quickly Father spoke. "I apologize for my daughter. I'm sure she didn't mean to criticize." He introduced the family and explained that they had just landed in America.

The doctor in turn apologized for stopping. He smiled as he held out his hand to Father. "I've never made such informal introductions before, but these are unusual times. Perhaps the ladies will forgive us." He tipped his hat.

"Is the worst of the epidemic over, Doctor?" Father asked.

"Yes. It was at its worst in the hot weather of August. We hope soon that it will be over."

Bessie looked at the doctor. How hard he must have worked these past months!

"I wish we could find a cure for cholera," he went on, "but first we must find out what causes it." He glanced anxiously toward the hospital. Then he turned back toward Father. "Perhaps someday we will. Or perhaps one of your youngsters, Mr. Blackwell, will win the fight over such diseases." The doctor smiled at Bessie. With a wave of his hand, he hurried on his way.

Once again Father started off. The family followed close behind. Soon they found themselves at the City Hotel.

Father thanked Ted for his help. Then he gave him a handful of copper coins. "For a new ball," Father said with a wink.

Ted's eyes grew big. "I've never had this much money before—all for myself. Thank you, Mr.

Blackwell!" He wished his new friends well and promised to return and visit them.

Within a short time the family was comfortably settled in the hotel. Father set to work at once to arrange his business affairs and find a house for the family.

One day, two weeks after they had arrived in America, Father returned with exciting news.

"I've found a house for us," he announced with obvious pleasure.

The children shouted with joy. Mother said that now they would feel much more settled.

"A house of our very own in America!" Bessie cried. "Now our adventure in a new land can really begin!"

So, with much enthusiasm, the Blackwells moved into their new home in America at 93 Thompson Street.

The Rescue

THE BREEZE from the ocean was cool, and the damp salt air felt good to Bessie. She stooped and ran her fingers through the coarse pale sand of the beach.

"How nice it is to be out in the country!" thought Bessie. Father had rented an old farmhouse in Rockaway, Long Island, for the summer. Though the house was somewhat shabby, it was large enough and roomy. And the Blackwells found the ocean breezes refreshing. The summer's heat in New York was worse than any they had known in England.

They had been in America almost a year now.

Bessie's youngest brother—George Washington Blackwell—had been born last November, just a few weeks after they had landed.

Behind Bessie the surf thundered as high waves broke close to shore. "What fun this is!" Bessie thought. She and Emily, who was seven now, had the beach almost to themselves. There was just one other person that she could see—a young man, farther down the beach.

Bessie turned to see where her sister was. Emily was close to the water's edge. She waved to Bessie. Barefoot, she stooped in the damp sand. She, too, was collecting sea shells.

Bessie turned back and again dug into the dry sand. Her fingers struck a tiny object. Eagerly she pulled it out. It was a perfectly formed little snail shell. Happily she added it to the shells she held in her left hand.

It had been a long walk from the farm to the shore. But Bessie and Emily enjoyed their walks to the beach. Sometimes Anna and Marian came, too. Almost always Emily came to the beach when Bessie did.

"Bessie!" Emily called excitedly.

Bessie glanced around.

Emily was waving her hand. "There are a lot of shells down here!" She had worked her way out farther toward the water.

Bessie could see that the tide was just beginning to turn. It had been going out but now it was coming in. Close to the water's edge the sand stopped. Beyond, going out into the water, the beach was stony.

The tide had left behind many different kinds of shells wedged in the stones. Yet Bessie chose to look for her shells farther up on the beach. Perhaps she wouldn't find as many shells as Emily, but she hoped she might find a rare or unusual shell hidden in the sand.

Emily worked her way out among the small

slippery stones. Eagerly she bent over and picked up a shell—then another and another. She gathered her long skirts in one hand and held them up, out of reach of the water. Then she put her shells into the lap of her skirts.

Emily was so busy she forgot how close she was to the breakers. She'd turned her back to the ocean and didn't see the surf foam and swirl about her. As she worked, it came in closer and closer. The water washed around her feet, but Emily seemed to be deaf to the thunder of the great waves breaking behind her.

Bessie, too, was so busy with her shells that she noticed little else. Her keen eyes found many tiny shells half buried in the sand. Suddenly out of the corner of one eye Bessie saw a great wave come rushing in. It was far bigger and faster than any she had seen earlier. Alarmed, she saw that Emily was much too close to where the wave would break.

"Emily," she cried, "watch out!" But before Bessie could finish the warning, the great wave broke just behind Emily.

Emily's back was turned to it. The water rushed over the stones and rose rapidly to above her knees. Then the force of the wave shoved her forward. With a cry, she lost her balance. Her seashells flew in every direction.

Bessie ran toward Emily as fast as she could. At the same time a young man dashed out onto the wet sand and stones. He was far ahead of Bessie and reached Emily first. Quickly he picked her up and carried her back to the safety of the dry sand.

Bessie saw that it was the same young man she had seen walking on the beach earlier.

"Are you all right, Emily?" asked Bessie anxiously.

Emily nodded her head. Her reddish hair glistened in the hot August sun. "Yes—I think

114

so." She looked down at her soaked skirts. The top part of her dress was splashed, too. "But I'm a little wet," she added.

Bessie couldn't help laughing. "You look it, Emily." Then, with a smile, Bessie turned to the young man. She guessed that he was just a few years older than Anna. "Thank you, sir."

He grinned and bowed low to Bessie. "I was happy to be of service to you young ladies. My name is Robert Dunn."

Bessie had heard the name Dunn before. "Perhaps I've heard it from Mother," she thought. She introduced herself and Emily. She told him that they were spending the summer at Rockaway, and she explained where the farmhouse was located.

"Why, we are neighbors!" the young man said, surprised. "My parents have a house not far down the road from yours."

Now Bessie recalled where she had heard

115

the name Dunn lately. Earlier in the summer Mother had been invited to have tea with Mrs. Dunn, Robert's mother.

Emily stood quietly while Bessie talked. Then suddenly tears came to her eyes. She sniffled.

"What's wrong, Emily?" Bessie asked.

"My seashells!" Emily looked sorrowfully at Bessie, as two large tears ran down her cheeks. "I was so excited I forgot—I lost them when I fell into the water."

Young Mr. Dunn stooped down. He reached into the pocket of his coat and pulled out a large handful of shells.

"Oh!" Emily sighed, as she looked at his shells. "You have a lot of pretty ones!"

"I'll share them with you," he offered with a smile. He pointed up the beach. There were two large rocks sticking out of the sand. "We'll go sit on those rocks and divide the shells between the two of us.

116

Emily wiped her tears away and smiled.

Bessie offered to share her shells, too. The warm sun would dry Emily's clothes quickly, before they started home. And they would have a chance to get to know their neighbor.

He seemed like a very nice young man, Bessie thought. Now that she had talked with him she didn't feel at all shy. Usually she found it very hard to talk with someone she didn't know.

As they sat on the rocks, they sorted the shells. Mr. Dunn told the girls he was in medical school. "In one more year," he said with a grin, "you may call me 'Doctor.' "

Emily giggled. "I'm going to call you 'Doctor' from now on—'Doctor Bob.' I like you."

The time passed quickly. Bessie asked Doctor Bob many questions about medical school. She listened, fascinated, as he told her about the subjects he studied.

"Anatomy," he explained, "is the study of the

human body." He said he had to learn the names of all the bones and muscles and where the organs of the body were.

"What are those?" Emily wanted to know, wrinkling her nose.

He grinned. "Well, your stomach and heart, for example. Each one is an organ."

"Go on," Bessie urged. "What else do you learn about?"

Doctor Bob laughed. "So many things—I couldn't begin to tell you all of them in a day. But I'll try to give you a general idea."

He went on to say that the medical students learned the names of all the diseases. Then they learned how to find out what was wrong with a patient.

"So we study symptoms—that is, the signs of trouble in the human body. Symptoms—like a headache or a stomachache—tell the doctor what's wrong with the patient."

It all sounded very challenging to Bessie. One would certainly have to study and work very hard to become a doctor.

"After we find out what's wrong with the patient," Doctor Bob said, "then we treat him. Sometimes we operate. This is called surgery. Sometimes we can treat him with medicine."

Doctor Bob paused and looked at his pocket watch. It was almost four o'clock. The girls were surprised to learn it was so late.

"We must hurry home," Bessie said. "Mother and Father will wonder where we are."

"I'll be glad to drive you," Doctor Bob offered. "I have my horse and buggy here. It's a fairly long walk home, and I don't want Emily to lose her shells again." He laughed.

Bessie and Emily happily accepted his offer. Carefully Bessie tied her shells in her handkerchief. Emily did the same. Then they climbed up the sand bank to the road.

Doctor Bob had hitched his horse to a nearby tree. He helped the girls into the buggy, and soon they were on their way home.

When they reached the Blackwell home, Doctor Bob helped the girls down. Bessie thanked him for the ride, and Emily thanked him for the lovely seashells.

"Now what will Mother and Father and Aunt Bar say about my clothes?" Emily asked. With a worried look she turned to Bessie. "I was having such a good time, I forgot about falling in the ocean."

Bessie smiled at Emily. "If we tell them all that happened, I think they'll understand. It was an accident that you fell in."

Doctor Bob laughed. "Yes, Emily. And, after all, you were rescued by a neighbor. So it all came out fine in the end."

Suddenly Bessie had an idea. "Why don't you stay for tea, Doctor Bob? I know Mother and

Father would be pleased. And we should do something for you—for rescuing Emily."

"Well——" Doctor Bob began.

Just then Father appeared on the porch.

"Father!" Emily called excitedly. "Come meet Doctor Bob—our neighbor."

With a smile, Father joined the group. Bessie introduced Doctor Bob, who shook hands with Father. She told Father where they had met.

Emily interrupted Bessie. "I'll tell him how we met," she said, a serious look on her face.

Emily told Father the story of how she slipped on the stones and fell into the ocean. She explained that Doctor Bob came to her rescue. Then he drove them home.

"Could he stay for tea, Father?" Emily asked at the end of her story.

Father laughed. "Yes, of course. We'd be happy if you would join us," he said, turning to Doctor Bob.

Doctor Bob accepted the invitation, and with a flurry of excitement, the girls led him into the parlor of the house.

When the family heard Emily's story, the children laughed. Aunt Bar agreed that Emily's name should not be put in the Black Book she kept this time.

"Experience is a good teacher, Emily," Father added. "Now you have learned how strong the waves are. Next time you will be more careful and stay well out of their reach."

"Yes, Father," Emily answered. "I won't forget what happened today."

"And neither will I," added Bessie, smiling at Doctor Bob. She was thinking of all the exciting things he had told her about medical school. "How wonderful it would be to be a doctor!" she thought. "Just think of all the people Doctor Bob will help! His life's work will be really important."

After a while Doctor Bob said that he must be getting home. He told Bessie and Emily and the other Blackwells good-by and promised to call again soon.

"If you ever need help, Emily," he teased, "just let me know." Then he waved and drove off in his buggy.

A Call For Help

EAGERLY BESSIE saddled Blackie. It was a beautiful day for a ride, Bessie thought.

The Blackwells kept three horses and a pony at the Rockaway farm. The pony, Ginger, was for the younger children to ride. Anna, Marian, Bessie, and Sam were permitted to ride the horses whenever they wished.

"Perhaps," Bessie said to herself, "Doctor Bob will come and ride with us one day. What fun that would be!" Just a few days had passed since they met at the seashore, but Bessie was eager to see him again. He was so nice and so friendly, and he was one of the few people

124

she knew at their Rockaway home outside of her own family.

She patted Blackie's shining coat. She had brushed him down good before putting the saddle on. Anna once complained that this should be the boys' job. But Father said that if the girls rode the horses, they should also learn to take care of them.

Bessie liked to curry—comb and brush—Blackie. He stood very still while she worked on him. Occasionally he would snort and nod his head, as if to thank her for making him look so splendid.

Soon Bessie was ready to go. Anna and Marian had decided to work in the garden this afternoon. Samuel had gone into the city with Father for the day. The younger children were romping in the daisy-filled meadow behind the farmhouse.

Ginger was tethered back there. She was tied

to a long rope. The rope was fastened to a stake in the ground. This gave her plenty of room to trot and prance and play.

Bessie looked toward the meadow. The pony seemed to be having as good a time as the children. She ran back and forth, tossing her blonde mane. Her reddish-brown coat glistened in the bright sun.

Bessie smiled as she thought of how much the younger children loved Ginger. Sarah Ellen and Howard toddled after Emily and Henry, who were playing tag. Ginger raced after them.

With a final glance toward the meadow, Bessie mounted Blackie and rode off down the dirt road. She rode Blackie as often as she could. She was a good rider, too. Father said she was the best rider of all the Blackwells. This is why he let her ride alone whenever she wanted to take Blackie out.

After an hour had passed, Bessie turned

Blackie toward home. Her cheeks were flushed with the excitement and thrill of the ride.

She'd traveled in a wide circle and was now near the farm. As she rode into the barnyard she was met by eight-year-old Henry.

His eyes were wide and frightened-looking as he ran to meet her.

What could have happened? Bessie wondered. Quickly she slid down from Blackie.

"Bessie! Bessie!" Henry cried. "Something terrible has happened to Ginger." Henry's words came in a rush. "She stumbled, out in the meadow, and now she can't get up."

Bessie's heart gave a jump. What if Ginger had broken her leg? If so, she couldn't ever be ridden again. She'd be taken away. How sad the younger children would be!

Bessie hoped that this wasn't true. Perhaps Ginger wasn't hurt badly, but she knew she must hurry and find out.

She hitched Blackie to a post near the barn. Then she followed Henry out to the meadow.

Ginger lay quietly in the long grass. Her head rested in Emily's lap. Emily gently stroked Ginger's sleek coat. The little girl's eyes were filled with tears. Sarah Ellen and Howard crouched sad-eyed and silent beside her.

Emily looked up. "Oh, Bessie!" she cried. "What shall we do?"

Bessie tried not to show her fears. "When did Ginger hurt herself?" she asked.

"Just a few minutes ago," Henry answered. "It's her right front leg," he added.

Bessie knelt down beside the pony. She looked at Ginger's leg. She couldn't see anything wrong with it, but Ginger raised her head when Bessie touched it down near the hoof.

What should she do? Bessie asked herself. Father was in the city, and Mother was busy with the baby. "A doctor could tell us what to do—he could help us," Bessie said, thinking out loud. Suddenly she cried, "I know!"

The younger children looked hopefully toward their older sister.

"I'll get Doctor Bob. I'm sure he'll be able to help Ginger!"

"Oh, Bessie!" cried Emily. "That's a wonderful idea." Then her smile disappeared. "But do you think he'd come—just to see a pony?"

"I'm sure he'll understand and come," she said. Maybe a pony wasn't a very important patient, Bessie realized. But Ginger was very important to them.

"Henry," Bessie went on, "I think you should tell Mother what has happened. Please tell her I've gone over to the Dunns', so that she will know where I am."

"What can I do, Bessie?" asked Emily.

"You can stay with Ginger," Bessie answered. It would be best, she thought, if the pony stayed where she was. If they tried to get her to her feet, they might hurt her leg some more.

Ponies, Bessie knew, could sometimes be very stubborn—especially Ginger. Father said Ginger had a mind of her own. If Ginger didn't want to stand—even if she could—she wouldn't, Bessie thought.

"You can call Anna or Marian if you need any help while I'm gone," Bessie added.

130

Then she ran back to get Blackie. Soon she was on her way to the Dunns'. They lived about a mile from the Blackwells. Their large white house was set well back from the dirt road. Doctor Bob had told her where the house was. She had passed it many times on her rides through the countryside.

She rode hard and fast, urging Blackie to gallop. Within a short time, she reached the Dunns', but the house looked quiet. There was no one in the yard, and the barn door was open.

"What if no one is home?" she thought anxiously.

Quickly she hitched Blackie to a post near the house. She ran to the front door and knocked. She waited for what seemed like a very long time. Then finally she heard steps within.

She was hopeful that it was Doctor Bob. But the door swung open and she was greeted by a tall pleasant-looking lady.

"May I speak to Doctor Bob, please?" Bessie said with difficulty. She was still a little breathless from her ride. "I'm Elizabeth Blackwell."

The lady smiled. "Why you must be Bessie! My son Robert has told me about you—and your sister Emily. Won't you come in?"

"No, thank you, Mrs. Dunn." As briefly as she could, Bessie explained to Mrs. Dunn what had happened. "We thought Doctor Bob might help us with Ginger."

Mrs. Dunn shook her head. "I'm sorry, Bessie. Robert went out for a drive earlier this afternoon. Perhaps he will be home soon." Then she paused, thoughtful. "I could give him the message." She smiled warmly. "I'm sure he'll help you."

Bessie smiled back at Mrs. Dunn. Now she felt really sure that Doctor Bob would come. If only he would come home soon!

"Thank you, Mrs. Dunn," she said. As she rode from the yard, she waved good-by.

Though Bessie was anxious to get home, she let Blackie take his time. She knew he was tired and hot from the fast ride to the Dunns'.

When she rode into the yard at home, Henry was there to meet her.

"Where's Doctor Bob?" he asked.

"He will come—soon, I hope," Bessie answered. As she unsaddled Blackie, she told Henry of her talk with Mrs. Dunn. She put Blackie in his stall. Then she and Henry hurried out to the meadow.

When Bessie saw Emily and Ginger, she stopped still, surprised. Ginger was on her feet!

Bessie ran toward Emily.

"Oh, Bessie!" Emily cried happily. "Ginger got to her feet all by herself—just after you left. Isn't that wonderful!"

"Yes," Bessie answered with a smile. Yet, she noticed, Ginger held her right hoof off the ground as she stood.

"I didn't have a chance to tell you," Henry explained. "We kept Ginger down here in the meadow because we thought we should keep her quiet until you returned."

"Perhaps," said Bessie thoughtfully, "if we lead her slowly, we can get her safely to the barn. At least, now we know her leg isn't broken."

"How do we know?" Henry looked puzzled.

"Ginger wouldn't be able to get to her feet if her leg was broken," Bessie said.

"Good old Ginger!" Emily happily patted the pony's neck.

Cheered by the thought that Doctor Bob would be along soon, Bessie, Emily, and Henry led Ginger to the barn.

Just as they reached the barn, Bessie saw a cloud of dust far down the dirt road. Soon she could see that the dust was raised by a fast-moving buggy. As it drew close, she saw that it was Doctor Bob's buggy.

"Hurrah!" Henry shouted.

Emily jumped up and down. "Doctor Bob! Doctor Bob!" she called.

Happily Bessie ran to meet him. "I'm so glad you came right away!"

He grinned. "I came as soon as I got your message, Bessie. Now, where is the patient?"

Bessie took Doctor Bob to Ginger. Henry had led her into her stall. The children were so glad to see Doctor Bob that they all talked at once.

Expertly Doctor Bob examined Ginger's leg. When he had finished, he straightened up and looked at the children. "She'll be as good as new in a few weeks," he said with a smile. "She's just strained a muscle or tendon in her leg. But it's not bad."

"Oh, I'm so glad that she will be all right!" Emily cried.

Henry shouted the good news. Bessie smiled broadly at the doctor.

"Thank you, Doctor Bob, for coming," Bessie said gratefully.

"I was happy I could help." Then he threw back his head and laughed. "Wait until the fellows at medical school hear that my first patient was a pony!"

Then everyone laughed.

"Now," said Doctor Bob, "I'll bind up Ginger's leg, so that she can walk on it. The binding will help to make it heal faster."

He took some material that had been wrapped in a ball from his pocket. "When I heard that Ginger's leg had been hurt, I brought this along," he explained.

"Why didn't Ginger get up after she stumbled?" Bessie questioned the doctor as she watched him work. "You said she hadn't hurt her leg very much."

Doctor Bob wound the two-inch cloth strip around and around the lower part of the pony's

136

leg. At Bessie's question, he grinned and shook his head. "I don't know. Ginger probably could have got up right away if she wanted to. Maybe she was just too frightened to try. Or maybe she was just too comfortable—with her head in Emily's lap!"

Emily giggled at Doctor Bob's joke, and Henry laughed.

"Ginger sure is an independent pony," he said.

"Father says she takes that after us Blackwells," Emily said with another giggle.

In a few minutes Doctor Bob had the lower part of the pony's leg neatly bound. "I'll come back and take the binding off when I'm sure the leg has healed."

Bessie, Emily, and Henry thanked him again for coming. He grinned and with a wave of his hand drove off in his buggy.

Late that afternoon Father and Samuel returned from the city. When all the family was together, Bessie told them about Doctor Bob's first patient.

"You were a quick thinker, Bessie," Father said, "to go to Doctor Bob for help."

"He said he would come if we ever needed him," Emily put in, excitedly, "and Ginger did need him today."

"Doctor Bob is a very nice young man," Mother said. "I'm sure he'll make a very good doctor. No one's need or call for help will ever go unanswered by him. That's what makes a really good doctor."

Bessie thought about Mother's words. Yes, she understood what Mother meant. Doctor Bob would give his patients more than medicine. He would treat them with love, kindness, and understanding, too.

The Dancing Party

IT WAS SHORTLY after midnight. Fifteen-year-old Bessie sat on the edge of her bed. She rubbed tallow on her icy hands, which were red and numb from the cold. The ride home from New York on the ferry boat had been a chilly one. Bessie's warm flannel nightgown felt good.

Two years had passed now since the Blackwells had moved from New York City to the little town of Paulus Hook, New Jersey. Their new home was directly across the Hudson River from New York. Bessie thought it was fun to be living in the country once again.

Many of the townspeople were farmers. They

lived in old Dutch stone houses. Pigs, sheep, and ducks roamed at will over the unfenced country-side nearby. Fishermen and farmers lived side by side.

Every day, despite the weather, Bessie and her brothers and sisters traveled to New York to school. They traveled on the ferryboat that went back and forth across the Hudson River.

Several times this past winter the river had been solidly frozen. Only then did the Black-well children stay home from school. Henry made the most of these unexpected holidays. But Bessie kept up her studies at home until the ice broke and they were able to travel once again into the city.

Bessie, Anna, and Marian spent many eve-nings in the city. Sometimes they stayed over-night with their aunts who had remained in New York when the Blackwells moved to Paulus Hook. Most of the time, however, they caught the last ferry home near midnight. They went to sewing circles, political meetings, and literary evenings at Mrs. Gautier's on Greenwich Street.

This evening Bessie, Anna, and Marian had been in to hear the famous Fanny Wright speak. Miss Wright talked on equal rights for women. Women, she said, should be able to vote. They should be given equal rights with the men.

With a bounce, Anna sat down beside Bessie on the bed. "Miss Wright's talk was so inspiring!" she said enthusiastically. "It made my head whirl with excitement!" She hesitated, then added, "How can you be so calm, Bessie, after tonight?"

Bessie glanced at her oldest sister. Father called Anna the "family firebrand." She was dark, thin, excitable. "How different we are!" Bessie said to herself.

"I do think Miss Wright is a very unusual woman," she replied aloud.

142

"Oh, yes, indeed!" Marian interrupted as she joined her two sisters. She tilted her pretty head and looked up at the ceiling. "When I get married, I'm going to have *all* daughters. And I'm going to teach them to believe in equal rights for women. That will help Miss Wright's cause!" she added proudly.

Anna's eyes flashed as she looked at her warm-hearted sister. "Well, I'm going to do something right away," she snapped. "I don't want to live a sheltered life—to depend on someone else to take care of me. I want the freedoms Miss Wright said we women deserve."

Bessie listened closely as Anna spoke. Her sister, she knew, was sometimes moody and hard to get along with. But she was almost grown up, and she was very smart.

Marian looked hurt. "But what else can we do, Anna?"

Anna's eyes glittered with purpose. "I'll do

something—like write a famous book. Or maybe I'll become a famous musician. If women can prove that they're just as smart as men, they'll earn their equal rights." She paused and glanced at Bessie. "Perhaps I should concentrate on writing. Bessie plays the piano better than any of us—she could be the famous musician."

Bessie looked down at her hands. The fingers were strong. When she played, they flew over the keys of the piano—fast and sure of each note.

She smiled to herself and shook her head. No —she loved to play the piano, but she didn't want to be a musician.

"What do you want to do, Bessie?" Marian asked eagerly.

Bessie looked thoughtful. "I'm not sure," she answered. "I'd like to do something really hard —something that's never been done before."

Suddenly their talk was interrupted by a tap on the door. Mother, in her robe, came in.

"Such chattering that's going on in here!" she said with a smile. "It's long after midnight. Time for you girls to be asleep!"

"Yes, Mother," they answered.

"Don't forget," Mother went on, "tomorrow evening is the dancing party. My friend, Mrs. Gregory, is looking forward to you girls being there. You'll want to be rested and look your prettiest. And, Bessie, this will be your first grown-up dancing party."

When Bessie thought of the party, she felt frightened. There would be so many people there that she didn't know, and most of the guests would be Anna's age—almost grown up. What if none of the boys asked her to dance? How awful she would feel! She was certain she would be a failure. Mrs. Gregory had invited her specially, so that she could be with Anna and Marian.

Bessie looked at her two pretty sisters. "I'll

always be plain-looking," she said to herself. "And I know I'll never be popular like Anna or Marian." With a sigh, she hung her head.

"Why, Bessie, what's wrong?" Mother asked.

"I—I don't really want to go to the party," she answered. "It just won't be any fun for me."

"Of course it will!" Mother cried with enthusiasm. "You have a beautiful new dress to wear, and you're a very good dancer. Now, no more nonsense. Into bed with you."

Even so, thought Bessie as she climbed into bed, she was sure not to have a good time at the dance. "A pretty dress doesn't make a pretty girl," she said to herself.

It seemed to Bessie that Anna and Marian spent the entire day getting ready for the dance. Anna brushed her hair until it shone, and Marian spent hours curling hers on a rounded stick.

Mother helped Bessie into her new dress. It had tiny hoops in the skirt and a long row of

146

tiny buttons down the back. Bessie didn't have the patience to fuss over how she looked.

When Mother finished with the dress, Bessie looked in the mirror. "Oh, it is a pretty dress!" Bessie admitted. The color was just right.

Early in the evening the three girls arrived at Mrs. Gregory's. She lived in a large stone house in the city.

After greeting Mrs. Gregory, Bessie followed her two sisters into the large drawing room. The young men and women sat on or stood near the chairs that lined the walls of the room. In a corner, at the far end of the room, was the piano.

Bessie felt her cheeks grow hot as she glanced around the room. Most of the people were strangers to her. But there were a few boys and girls Marian's age that she recognized.

She followed close behind her sisters. They joined a small group of girls at the near end of the room. Soon they were talking and laughing together—all except Bessie. She sat stiffly on the edge of her chair.

"Does my dress look all right?" she wondered. "What shall I do when the dance begins?"

Suddenly her thoughts were interrupted. The music had started. She saw Mrs. Gregory moving gracefully around the room. Smiling and nodding, Mrs. Gregory signaled that the dance was to begin.

Bessie looked down at her hands folded in her lap. She was afraid to look up. Surely none of the boys would come her way. There were so many pretty girls for them to choose from.

"Bessie!" Anna whispered, giving her a nudge. "Smile. No one will ask you to dance if you look like a frightened mouse!"

Bessie's cheeks burned at Anna's words, but she knew Anna's advice was well meant.

Then, out of the corner of her eye, she saw that Anna had whirled out onto the dance floor.

Her partner was tall and dark—one of the best-looking young men at the dance.

Marian had been asked to dance, too. Bessie saw that her sisters were having a wonderful time. The man at the piano was playing a waltz. Bessie forgot that she was alone as she listened to the music. She nodded her head and hummed softly. Music made her forget how shy she felt.

She didn't notice that a boy came up to one side of her chair. "M-may I have this dance?" he asked.

Surprised, Bessie looked up at him. He was not much older than she. He had freckles, and his ears stuck too far out from his head.

Bessie smiled at him. Maybe he felt as shy as she did. He certainly wasn't good looking.

"My name is Alfred—Alfred Drake."

"And mine is Bessie Blackwell."

He blushed. "I—I like to waltz," he stammered. "Do you, Bessie?"

"Yes," she answered with a smile.

Soon they were whirling and dancing along with the other couples. Bessie was happy that Alfred was an excellent dancer. He led her through some of the more difficult dance steps smoothly and easily. With each step Bessie grew more sure of herself. She forgot how she had dreaded the dancing party. "Why this is fun after all!" she thought to herself.

When the dance was finished, Alfred led Bessie back to her chair. Mrs. Gregory, who had been standing by, spoke to them.

"What wonderful dancers you two are!" she said enthusiastically.

"Bessie is the best partner I've ever had," Alfred said proudly. Then he turned to Bessie. "Will you dance with me again later, Bessie?"

"I'd be happy to," Bessie answered.

After Alfred left, Mrs. Gregory asked Bessie if she was enjoying herself.

"Oh, yes, thank you, Mrs. Gregory!" Bessie said politely.

"Your sisters tell me," Mrs. Gregory went on, "that you're very good at playing the piano. I wonder, Bessie, if you would please play for the next waltz? I'd so like to hear you, and I know the boys and girls would enjoy it, too."

Bessie had admired Mrs. Gregory's great piano. It was one of the best she'd ever seen. What fun it would be to play it! And she knew by heart the music for several waltzes.

Yet as Bessie thought of playing before so many people, her fingers turned cold with fear. She'd played at home many times for the family, but never in front of so many strangers.

It wouldn't be polite to refuse, Bessie thought to herself. Somehow, despite her fear, she must make herself do what Mrs. Gregory asked.

"I'll—I'll try, Mrs. Gregory," Bessie answered after a moment.

Her heart pounding hard, Bessie followed Mrs. Gregory to the far end of the room. When the music for the second dance had ended, Mrs. Gregory clapped her hands.

The young people stopped talking and turned to see what Mrs. Gregory wanted.

"Ladies and gentlemen," she announced, "as a special favor Miss Bessie Blackwell will play the next waltz for us." She smiled at Bessie and motioned toward the piano.

Mr. Jameson, the pianist, stood and bowed to Bessie.

Nervously Bessie smoothed her skirts. She was afraid to look at the audience. Quickly she sat down at the piano. Her hands shook as she held them out toward the keys. "I *must* not be afraid," she told herself firmly. "Once I start to play, I'll forget about being scared. I must pretend I'm at home, playing for the family."

With determination, she started to play. Soon

152

everyone was dancing to the happy melody of the waltz. Gradually Bessie's nervousness disappeared. She forgot she was among strangers. She thought only of the music. The piece was a difficult one, but she knew the notes well. The powerful tone of the great piano thrilled her.

After she struck the last chord, there was loud applause. Anna and Marian rushed toward the piano and hugged Bessie.

"Oh, you played beautifully, Bessie!" Anna told her sister.

"And you didn't miss a note," Marian added excitedly.

The other young people gathered close around Bessie. Their praise made Bessie blush. "I don't think I've ever been happier!" Bessie thought to herself. "This is such fun."

For the rest of the evening Bessie did not lack for dancing partners. One after another of the boys asked her to dance.

When the dancing was over, Mrs. Gregory served ice cream, cakes, and lemonade.

"Oh, what a happy surprise this evening has been!" Bessie told Anna and Marian.

Her sisters laughed with her.

"Just wait till Mother hears that you were the belle of the ball!" Anna said.

A Long Journey West

CLOUDS OF SMOKE and cinders came through the open windows of the railroad car. But seventeen-year-old Bessie didn't mind the noise and the dirt this bright May morning.

What a thrill to ride the railroad—all the way to Philadelphia! she thought. Father said that one day it might run as far west as Cincinnati. This was to be the Blackwells' new home.

Aunt Bar had called the railroad a "mad new invention." But Aunt Mary—the one aunt who had decided to move west with the family—said bravely that she was not afraid to ride it.

Bessie glanced across the aisle. Her mother

seemed to be enjoying the train ride. She had been reading. But now she laid aside the book of sermons and watched the fast-changing landscape. Despite the dirt of the train, Mother's new summer straw bonnet looked gay and fresh. Somehow, Bessie thought, Mother always looked dignified, yet kind and gentle. Her hair was still black and glossy, though Father's was turning gray.

Father's fortunes in the sugar business had failed in New York, so he had decided to move his family to Ohio. There he planned to start another sugar refinery. Business, he said, would be much better near the new frontier.

Bessie looked forward to this move as a great new adventure. Yet she couldn't hold the tears back as she said good-by to Anna and Marian. For the first time, they were to be parted. Anna went to Burlington, Vermont, to teach, and Marian was teaching in New York.

The Blackwells reached Philadelphia late in the morning.

"Come along, everyone," Father said, as he helped Mother off the train. "We must see as much of Philadelphia today as possible. We must make the most of our trip west—and see as many sights as we can."

"What makes Philadelphia so special? Why is it any different from New York?" young Howy wanted to know.

"Why, Howy, Philadelphia is the home of American independence!" Father answered. Then he added with a smile, "I'll show you— right after lunch."

Father took rooms for the family at the hotel. Bessie welcomed the chance to freshen up after the train ride. Father said they would spend the night here, then they would continue their journey tomorrow morning.

"Now," Father announced after they had had

lunch, "we'll find out what makes Philadelphia such a famous city."

"Where are we going first, Father—to Independence Hall?" Henry asked.

"No, Henry, we'll save that till last," Father said. "First we'll see one of the most unusual sights in America today."

"What is it—what is it?" the younger children asked excitedly.

"You'll see!" Smiling, Father led them along the tree-lined paved streets of the city.

"Everything seems so nice and clean here," Bessie said admiringly. "And there are lovely parks everywhere!"

"You would notice how clean it is, Bessie," Sam teased, with a grin.

"Cities should be kept clean," Bessie replied firmly. "It isn't healthy for people to live in so much dirt—like they do in New York." Suddenly Bessie realized they had reached a river.

"This is the Schuykill River," Father explained. "And here is what I promised to show you—the Fairmont Water Works. These are the first water works in America."

From the long brick-paved terrace of the water works, Bessie could see the great dam and the stone mill building.

Sam was much impressed by the huge water wheels. They were made of wood and cast iron.

Henry, Bessie noticed, seemed most interested in the men who were fishing along the banks of the river.

The most thrilling sight of the afternoon for Bessie and Henry was Independence Hall. Howy said the Liberty Bell was the biggest he had ever seen.

Proudly Emily explained to Howy, Sarah Ellen, and Washy why the hall was so important. "On the fourth of July, 1776, the leaders of America adopted the Declaration of Independence. The Declaration said that the people of America were not going to be ruled by England any more. And that's how the United States was born!"

"Very good, Emily," Mother said.

"Yes, indeed, Emily," Father added. "You've learned your history very well. And now that you've all seen Independence Hall, you'll be able to remember why this city's so famous."

Talking excitedly of the new sights they had seen, the Blackwells returned to the hotel. Bessie retired early, because Father said they had a long day ahead of them tomorrow. She wanted to be well rested, for she didn't want to miss seeing the countryside of Pennsylvania. She fell asleep, wondering what tomorrow would be like.

Early the next morning they boarded a stagecoach for Columbia. Much to Bessie's surprise, Father said they would travel all night, too.

The stagecoach bounced them roughly from

side to side. Every few minutes Washy wanted to know if they were near Cincinnati yet.

Bessie laughed. "We're still a long, long way from Ohio, Washy."

That night Bessie tried to sleep as best she could. But only the youngest children could sleep peacefully on the bouncing coach. When the gray of early morning came, Bessie felt stiff and sore from the rough ride.

A drizzling rain made it difficult to see out the coach windows. Every now and then, however, Bessie caught glimpses of a river. "This," she said to herself, "must be the Susquehanna River!"

Soon the coach stopped at an inn. The weary passengers had breakfast. The warm food made everyone feel better, and soon the Blackwells were eager to be on their way once more.

In spite of the chill and fog of the morning, Bessie watched the scenery with mounting excitement. The farther along they got on their journey, the wilder and more romantic the countryside seemed to her. There were thick forests and rolling hills all around such as she had never seen before.

Suddenly Henry leaned toward the window. "What's that?" he cried, pointing out the side.

The stagecoach was traveling at a faster pace now. It was passing a large covered wagon. The sides of the wagon were painted bright red.

"I've never seen anything like that before," said Henry.

"I know what it is!" Sam cried, staring hard at the great covered wagon. "It's a Conestoga wagon. Isn't it, Father?"

"Yes, Sam," Father answered. "It carries freight from Philadelphia to the West. We'll probably see more of these wagons as we travel westward today."

Not only did they see more Conestoga wagons,

but twice their stagecoach was passed by riders who thundered by on fast moving horses.

Washy wanted to know why the horses traveled so fast.

"Those riders carry the mail," Father said. "It must be delivered quickly."

The next day was the day Bessie had been looking forward to most. Early in the morning the family boarded a canal barge. It was Bessie's first barge trip. She was surprised to find so many passengers crowded onto such a long narrow boat. "Why, there must be over thirty people on this boat!" she said to herself.

The barge sat low in the water. There was one large cabin. It was in the center of the boat. The roof of the cabin was only a few feet from the deck.

"The barge is built as flat as possible," Father explained, "so that it can pass safely under the bridges over the canal."

Alongside the canal ran a path. This, Father went on to explain, was called the towpath. Two horses were hitched to the boat. The horses walked along the towpath, pulling the barge.

Sarah Ellen and Washy were not sure they liked to ride on the barge. They and Howy sat close to Bessie and Emily on the open deck. Father, Mother, and Aunt Mary settled themselves comfortably on the low cabin roof. Henry and Sam went exploring.

Slowly and smoothly the flat boat moved through the water.

Suddenly there came a cry from the helmsman who steered the barge. "Low bridge coming! Everybody duck!" Then he raised a horn to his lips and blew a long blast.

Bessie and the other passengers crouched low as the barge slipped under the bridge. The passengers on the cabin roof flattened themselves until the barge cleared the bridge.

Soon Henry and Sam had made friends with the helmsman. At the next low bridge, Sam blew the horn. Henry shouted, "Low bridge coming! Everybody duck!"

"Oh, isn't this exciting! This is the wildest country yet!" cried Emily. "We haven't passed any houses or settlements for hours."

Bessie agreed with Emily. It was a wilderness—a beautiful one.

Late that afternoon the travelers reached Hollidaysburg, at the foot of the Allegheny Mountains. Here they left the canal barge behind and traveled over the mountains. At noon the next day they reached Johnstown. Once again they boarded a canal barge and traveled on toward Pittsburgh.

Henry and Sam were eager to see the old fort at Pittsburgh. Father said it was at this fort that the French and English had fought. Both had wanted North America. The English had won.

"Are we almost there, Father?" Henry asked eagerly.

"We're about twelve miles from Pittsburgh," answered Father. "Tonight we'll sleep in a nice comfortable city hotel."

Mother smiled. "I'm looking forward to a good rest, and the children need one, too. I think even Bessie is tired—though she seems to have more energy left than anyone else."

Suddenly there came a cry from the helmsman. "Looks like trouble ahead!"

In the dim light of dusk, Bessie could see two barges ahead of them. They had stopped. Silently Bessie's barge drew close to the other two and came to a stop.

"What is it, Father?" Bessie wanted to know.

Father leaned over the low rail of the barge. Some of the passengers from the other barges had gone ashore.

"It looks like a break in the canal, Bessie,"

168

Father answered at last. "A large part of one of the towpaths has caved in. There's not enough room for the barges to go past."

"Oh, dear!" Mother cried. "How long will we be here?"

"I'll try to find out," Father said. "Bessie, please help your mother and aunt watch the younger children."

Within a short time Father was back. He shook his head as he looked at Mother. "I'm afraid we're in for a wait, dear."

The children gathered close to hear the news Father had brought back.

"The break is a bad one," he went on. "The first barge sent word ahead to Pittsburgh several hours ago. A steamboat will come up the Allegheny River and take all barge passengers down to Pittsburgh tonight."

"Hurrah! A ride on a steamboat!" shouted Henry. "Hurrah!"

"May we go watch for it to come, Father?"
Sam asked. "The helmsman told me the river
is nearby. It's right across this meadow behind
the trees at the far end of it."

By now it was dark. The moon had not yet
risen. Bessie could see the shadowy forms of
the other passengers on the shore. Some started
walking across the meadow toward the river.

"No, Sam," Father said. "We're all going to
sleep while we can. It will be a long, long time
before the steamboat comes."

"But, Father," Washy said in a worried tone,
"if we're all asleep, we might get left behind."

Father and Mother laughed.

"I'll see to it that we don't get left behind,
Washy," Father promised with a smile.

Within an hour the moon had risen. The night
air was clear and crisp. Hundreds of stars dotted
the sky.

Bessie could not sleep. So much had happened in the last few days! She'd seen so many new things! And each day of the journey had been filled with excitement. What would tomorrow be like—and the next day?

She leaned back on the roof of the cabin and looked up at the brightly shining stars. At last her eyes closed and she dozed off.

Shortly after midnight, Bessie woke with a start.

"Steamboat coming!" she heard the helmsman call. "Steamboat coming!"

Quickly Bessie wakened the other Blackwells. Father, too, had heard the helmsman's call. He gathered the luggage together. He carried the heavier pieces. Henry and Samuel helped with these, too. Mother, Aunt Mary, and Emily carried the lighter carpetbags.

Sleepily Sarah Ellen, Howy, and Washy followed Bessie ashore.

The walk through the meadow was a short one.

Soon the Blackwells were comfortably settled on the steamboat. The younger children were asleep in their berths before the boat started back down the river to Pittsburgh.

After the Blackwells reached Pittsburgh, they spent a day touring the city. To Bessie this city was the gateway to the rough western frontier she'd heard so much about. For here axes, nails, shovels, knives, saddles and harnesses, shoes, and window glass were made for the western settlers. These goods were loaded into flatboats, and from here started their journey to the frontier country. The boats brought pork, flour, molasses, sugar, tobacco, and cotton back to Pittsburgh.

The following morning, the Blackwells boarded another steamboat—the "Tribune." It was much larger and handsomer than the one they had ridden on two nights before.

Sarah Ellen was frightened by the noise of its great steam engines. But Sam and Henry set off at once to explore the boat. Its hull was painted red and black, and the large cabin area was a gleaming white. Father said the "Tribune" could carry one hundred and fifty passengers.

Late in the day Emily joined Bessie at the boat's railing. They marveled at the ever-changing scenery. The forested hills seemed wilder and more lonely than any they had seen so far.

"Oh, Bessie, look!" cried Emily as the boat rounded a bend in the river.

Ahead Bessie saw a landing on the left shore. The steamboat turned toward it and slowed down. In the clearing at the landing were a few rough-looking log cabins.

"Do people really live in those?" Emily asked.

Bessie laughed. "Of course, silly! Each family builds its cabin from the trees in these forests. It's a hard life. But someday this settlement may be a big city—maybe as important as Pittsburgh or Cincinnati."

A few settlers had gathered on the landing to welcome the steamboat. Their clothes were as rough-looking as their homes, but the tanned faces of the men and women were friendly.

Soon the steamboat had taken on a large load of wood. This wood was the fuel the boat burned. Once again they were on their way down the Ohio River.

The following day Bessie watched eagerly as they rounded each bend of the river. "Today," she thought, "we will be in Cincinnati!"

On this side of the Allegheny Mountains the trees and foliage of the forest were in full bloom. The air was soft and warm, and the sun burned Bessie's fair skin.

Several times the boat stopped to get more wood and to load on a few more passengers. Despite the new sights, the day seemed long to Bessie. She could think only of Cincinnati and their new home.

Suddenly in the middle of the afternoon the boat's whistle sounded shrilly. They rounded a large bend in the river.

"We're here!" shouted Henry and Sam.

The Blackwells crowded close to Bessie at the railing. There, climbing the hill up from the river, was the great city of Cincinnati.

Bessie knew right away she would like her new home. The city looked warm and friendly in the sun. The streets were wide and tree-lined, and the brick houses looked neat and clean.

"I just know wonderful things will happen to us here!" Bessie cried excitedly.

Elizabeth Is Accepted

Young Elizabeth Blackwell scarcely noticed the chilly drizzling rain. The November wind whipped over the lake and along the streets of Geneva, New York.

As Elizabeth walked rapidly toward the Geneva College Campus, she could think only of the unexplored world that lay ahead of her. For at last she had been accepted into a medical school. She was the first woman ever to be given this opportunity in the United States.

She felt a great sense of responsibility. She must not fail, she knew. "I will work hard," twenty-six-year-old Elizabeth told herself. "I will study hard and learn as much as I possibly can. I must do my best as a doctor—and as a woman."

Elizabeth knew she must prove that a woman could be a good doctor. If she succeeded, other women would be welcomed into medical schools. But what if she failed?

As she hurried along, she held her gray cloak shut tight against the chill. She thought of her sister Emily and smiled. Perhaps one day Emily would follow in her footsteps. Not long ago Emily had told Elizabeth that she, too, wanted to become a doctor. Elizabeth had promised to do everything she could to help Emily. But Emily was still young. She had many years of study ahead of her yet before she would be ready for medical school.

Within a few minutes, Elizabeth saw ahead of her the round dome of the medical building.

"How long it has taken me to get here!" Elizabeth said to herself. She thought of the many times when her dream of becoming a doctor had seemed hopeless. Medical school after medical school had refused her admission. But Elizabeth did not give up trying.

Patiently she wrote an endless number of letters to the schools. She listed the many subjects she had studied. Whenever she could she read books about medicine. Her friend, Dr. Dickson, had let her borrow freely from his medical library. He had told her to study Greek, so Elizabeth had done this, too.

Many of the colleges were impressed by Elizabeth's scholarship. She was far better prepared than many of the young men who attended these schools. Yet one by one the schools answered "No" to her request. None would allow a woman —no matter how smart—to enter its medical school.

Elizabeth had also asked important Philadelphia doctors for their help. She had called on them at their homes in Philadelphia. One listened with interest to Elizabeth's story. He tried to persuade his friends at the University of Pennsylvania to allow Elizabeth to go to the university's school. But again the answer was "No." Some of the doctors laughed at Elizabeth's plan. They said that no woman was capable of becoming a doctor.

Even if she was accepted, she knew she would have to pay her own way through school. Since Father's death, the Blackwells had had very little money. So for two years Elizabeth had taught school. She had saved her money until she had put back enough for the years she would spend in medical school.

Then the letter came for which she had longed. Elizabeth's determination was rewarded. And now, at last, her dream of medical school was about to come true.

Inside the Geneva medical school building, Elizabeth was met by the Dean, Dr. Lee.

"Welcome to Geneva, Miss Blackwell," said Dr. Lee.

Elizabeth noticed that Dr. Lee seemed nervous. Of course! It was a new experience for Dr. Lee, too. Elizabeth was to be his first woman student.

She smiled. "Thank you, Dr. Lee. It's a great honor for me to be able to come to your school."

She hoped her voice didn't show how nervous she felt. What would the classes be like? Would the young men make fun of her? Suddenly her mind was filled with questions, and she felt afraid and alone.

Then Dr. Lee spoke again. "You have missed the first five weeks of the term, but I'm sure you'll be able to make up the work quickly. You have an outstanding record as a student."

Elizabeth was encouraged by Dr. Lee's praise.

"Now," he went on with a smile, "if you'll please follow me, I'll show you to the lecture room. There I will introduce you to the other students."

Quickly Elizabeth followed him down the hall. The door to the lecture room stood ajar. From inside Elizabeth could hear laughter and much loud talking.

Dr. Lee asked her to wait outside. When he entered the room, the young men quieted down.

"Gentlemen," Dr. Lee announced, "today Miss Blackwell will join your class. You all had a part in bringing her here, for the faculty gave you an unusual opportunity. We let you vote on whether or not Miss Blackwell should be admitted to our school. Each one of you voted in favor of her entrance. Each one of you realized at the time that Geneva College would be admitting the first woman medical student in the history of the country. You deserve praise for helping to give her this rare opportunity."

Then Dr. Lee turned and left the lecture room. When he returned, Elizabeth was with him. "Gentlemen," he said, "I should like to present to you your new classmate, Miss Elizabeth Blackwell."

A respectful hush fell over the room as the quiet-mannered Elizabeth followed Dr. Lee to the platform. Though her heart still fluttered, Elizabeth felt her courage returning. The students wanted her as a classmate, and she must prove herself worthy of the honor.

At times Elizabeth had feared that this moment would never come, but now it was here. She knew that she *could* not fail. She could not disappoint those people who believed so deeply in her ability to succeed.

Years of Progress

WITH PRIDE Elizabeth glanced around the hospital room. For today—May 12, 1857—one of her greatest dreams had come true. Today was the official opening of the New York Infirmary for Women and Children.

Beside her stood her sister Emily. She, too, was now a doctor. On the other side of Elizabeth stood Dr. Marie Zakrzewska. Elizabeth had helped Marie to become a doctor. And, as she had promised, she had encouraged Emily through long years of medical training.

Now, under Elizabeth's firm leadership, they had succeeded in founding the infirmary. It was

184

the first of its kind in America—a hospital devoted to the care of women and children.

"Oh, Elizabeth, I thought this day would never come!" Emily turned to her sister. "Now we have our own hospital."

"It is difficult to believe." Elizabeth smiled. "It's been eight years since I graduated from medical school. And how discouraged I used to feel during those hard years! For a long time only a handful of patients came to me. Few people—even women—would trust a woman doctor to care for them."

"Yes," Marie put in. "But still you had the courage to go on. Because of you I am now a doctor, and Emily has graduated from Western Reserve in Cleveland, Ohio, and is now a skilled surgeon."

Elizabeth shook her head. "The credit for today's success belongs to all of us." As she looked around the room she saw many famous people and leading citizens of New York. Among them were Dr. Henry Ward Beecher. And there was Peter Cooper standing near one of the infirmary's new beds.

With her head held high, Elizabeth stepped forward to open the official ceremony. Modestly she reported the work that had been done in the past. She told of the hundreds of ill and needy who had been cared for in her dispensary. No patient had ever been refused help because of poverty. The dispensary had welcomed the women and children of the slums of New York, and all who had come for help had been given the best of care, whether or not they could pay for the services.

"The education of women in medicine is a new idea," Elizabeth went on. "And it takes time to prove that a new idea can be a valuable one. We hope, here at the infirmary, to continue this work. We must prove to medical men, as

186

well as to the public, the skill women can bring to the medical profession."

When Elizabeth finished speaking, there was much applause. Her friends knew she would do great work at the infirmary.

The years proved that Elizabeth's friends were right. Shortly after the infirmary was opened, every bed was filled. These patients had faith in the women doctors. Dr. Emily was the hospital's surgeon. Dr. Marie was the resident physician. She spent all her time at the infirmary. Dr. Elizabeth was the director.

Eight months after the infirmary opened, the doctors started a training program for nurses. Free courses lasting four months were offered.

"This will be another step forward for women," Elizabeth told Emily. "We must allow only the best to take the courses. Well-qualified doctors *and* nurses can make great improvements in the medical field."

The work at the infirmary settled into a smooth routine. Then Elizabeth began to think of what she could do outside the United States to educate women in medicine. She talked over this idea with Emily. Emily agreed that there was much pioneering work to be done outside the United States.

So in 1858 Elizabeth went on a lecture tour of England. As a result of her talks there, a movement was started to found a hospital in England—one like the New York Infirmary.

When Elizabeth returned to New York, she went to work on another new idea—a medical school for women. Abruptly her plans were interrupted, for war was declared—the War Between the States.

Elizabeth was saddened by the news of war. She knew that the hospital would be crowded in the days to come. Her plans for a medical school must wait.

Emily and Elizabeth were together when word came that the fighting had started at Fort Sumter in the South. Elizabeth recalled how, long ago, her father had spoken against slavery.

"Yes, I remember," said Emily. "Father thought it was very wrong for one person to own another as a slave. He said every man should be free. Yet it is sad that the Northern states and Southern states should go to war."

During the war years Elizabeth and Emily worked harder than ever. The infirmary was overflowing with patients. But finally the war came to an end. The slaves had been freed. Now Elizabeth could plan once again for her medical school for women.

Once more Elizabeth succeeded in making a dream come true. In November 1868, the college for women opened officially at the infirmary. Its standards were high. Elizabeth saw to this—she wanted the college to offer the best medical education possible. And she made sure each student was good enough to enter the school. Entrance examinations were given, and only the best women students were accepted.

Elizabeth taught a new course which every student was required to take. It was a course in hygiene. She taught the importance of cleanliness. Disease, she said, spread quickly in dirty slums, homes, or badly run hospitals. Much sickness could be prevented if people were taught the health-giving qualities of fresh air and sunshine, she thought.

Elizabeth was one of the pioneers in the field of hygiene. She felt doctors knew too little about it. Hospitals, she lectured, should be kept spotlessly clean.

Much of the rest of her life was devoted to this cause. She gave hundreds of lectures and wrote books on the subject of hygiene. Through her efforts great progress was made.

When Elizabeth saw her dreams come true in America, she decided to go to England once more. In England she would carry on her crusade for hygiene.

Elizabeth was an old lady when she saw her family in America for the last time. She visited Emily, who now lived in Maine. Together they celebrated Emily's eightieth birthday and talked over old times. Emily had retired from medical practice.

"It was time to retire, Elizabeth," she said with a smile. "We've done what we could. Just think —now there are over 7,000 women practicing medicine in the United States! How different it was when we were young!"

Elizabeth smiled and nodded. "Our lives have been busy. And we've seen our dreams come true."

Contented and happy the two sisters talked far into the night.